"You're pregnant," he said.

"Yes, I'm pregnant, okay? But that's my business, not yours." Sylvie tried to push past him, but he stepped in front of the door and kicked it shut. The sharp click echoed through the hot, quiet room.

"We're not done talking yet, Ms. Mitchell."

Her head shot up. For the first time she stared hard at him, forcing herself to notice every little detail of his handsome face. If circumstances had been different…

"Please excuse me, Mr. Cahill."

"Call me Jon. You're going to see a lot of me in the future."

She shot a sharp glare at his calm features, ignoring his smooth-as-silk voice.

He continued. "I'm not condemning you for carrying my brother's child. I'm just telling you I *will* be a part of its life."

Dear Reader,

Welcome to the New Year—and to another month of fabulous reading. We've got a lineup of books you won't be able to resist, starting with the latest CAVANAUGH JUSTICE title from RITA® Award winner Marie Ferrarella. *Dangerous Disguise* takes an undercover hero, adds a tempting heroine, then mixes them up with a Mob money-laundering operation run out of a restaurant. It's a recipe for irresistibility.

Undercover Mistress is the latest STARRS OF THE WEST title from multi-RITA® Award-winning author Kathleen Creighton. A desperate rescue leads to an unlikely alliance between a soap opera actress who's nowhere near as ditsy as everyone assumes and a federal agent who's finally discovered he has a heart. In *Close to the Edge*, Kylie Brant takes a bayou-born private detective and his high-society boss, then forces them onto a case where "hands off" turns at last into "hands on." In Susan Vaughan's *Code Name: Fiancée,* when agent Vanessa Wade has to pose as the fiancée of wealthy Nick Markos, it's all for the sake of national security. Or is it? Desire writer Michelle Celmer joins the Intimate Moments roster with *Running on Empty*, an amnesia story that starts at the local discount store and ends up…in bed. Finally, Barbara Phinney makes her second appearance in the line with *Necessary Secrets*, introducing a pregnant heroine and a sexy cop— but everyone's got secrets to hide.

Enjoy them all, then come back next month for more of the best and most exciting romantic reading around.

Yours,

Leslie J. Wainger
Executive Editor

Please address questions and book requests to:
Silhouette Reader Service
U.S.: 3010 Walden Ave., P.O. Box 1325, Buffalo, NY 14269
Canadian: P.O. Box 609, Fort Erie, Ont. L2A 5X3

Necessary Secrets

BARBARA PHINNEY

INTIMATE MOMENTS™

Published by Silhouette Books

America's Publisher of Contemporary Romance

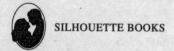 SILHOUETTE BOOKS

ISBN 0-373-27414-9

NECESSARY SECRETS

BARBARA PHINNEY

Barbara Phinney was born in England and raised in Canada. She has traveled throughout her life, loving to explore the various countries and cultures of the world. After she retired from the Canadian Armed Forces, Barbara turned her hand to romance writing. The thrill of adventure and the love of happy endings, coupled with a too-active imagination, have merged to help her create this and other wonderful stories. Barbara spends her days writing, building her dream home with her husband and enjoying their fast-growing children.

Dedicated to the soldiers and police officers
who have served on United Nations and
NATO peacekeeping missions around the world.

My story is not real, but the dangers these men and
women have faced are very real. They've kept the
peace—sometimes making it first—and they have made
those countries safer, especially for the children.

This author thanks them.

Chapter 1

The small town of Trail, Alberta, always bustled on a Friday. And with a sunny, early-June weekend advancing on the leading edge of a heat wave, the town hummed like a beehive when the canola bloomed.

Sylvie Mitchell parked her car and walked toward the local medical clinic, or more specifically, the small birthing clinic within it.

Sometime in December, she thought. Good timing, at least. With the ranch and campground at its slowest, she'd have more time for the baby.

And by then Andrea would have dragged Dad down to the condo in Mexico, and life would be quiet again.

After thirteen years in the Canadian Army, quiet sounded pretty good to Sylvie.

The squeal of tires cut through the stream of street noise, and she snapped her head around.

One burning, brutal memory bubbled to the surface....

The thick, wet Bosnian snow, the mess of rocks and brush

*and tree trunks, the strain of dirty brakes as her truck
skidded to a slushy stop barely in time. The jolting pop
of machine-gun fire. The cold wash of horror as she
watched Private Rick Cahill close his eyes for the last
time....*

A merry shout answered the squeal. Two teenagers,
cutting school, no doubt, threw greetings into Sylvie's
recollection, dissolving it. She blinked and hurried into
the clinic.

The receptionist smiled when she reached the counter.

"I need to see the doctor," she told the woman.

"Is it an emergency? We're booked until next
Wednesday."

"Wednesday's fine." Sylvie waited for the receptionist
to decide on a time.

The woman glanced up. "What seems to be the problem? Or is it for your yearly exam? I have to allot the
right amount of time."

Sylvie met the woman's gaze evenly. She'd seen her
around the grocery store and such, but the woman wasn't
a born-and-bred local. She may as well get used to stating
her condition. And seeing the look of surprise on the
faces of the few friends she had when they subtracted the
time she'd been home from how far along she was. "I'm
pregnant. Almost twelve weeks. I took a home-pregnancy
test this morning."

Her words sounded amazingly smooth, considering the
turmoil on which they'd ridden free.

What a shame she couldn't feel the same placidity
about the night of her baby's conception. Twelve weeks
ago, Rick had been alive. In Bosnia, in early spring. What
a terrible place and time to conceive a child.

Tears suddenly welled up and a thick lump of something ripened in her throat. *Oh, no! Not here.*

She continued to stare at the receptionist, an over-whelming horror swamping her as she realized she could break down at any moment. All those years running a quartermaster store, all that time in so many war zones, and now she was as tearful as a two-year-old.

"Here." The receptionist handed her a tissue.

Sylvie shook her head. "I don't need it. It's just the hormones. I don't cry." She wouldn't cry, either, not now, not ever. She'd been a soldier for thirteen years, done three tours of duty overseas and countless training exercises. She'd been the youngest warrant officer in her unit, and each promotion she'd earned was the result of hard work, not tears.

Besides, she had the baby to think about—the only thing left of the man who'd known the risks and had still made love to her.

She turned her head and drew a stabilizing breath. The "man." Who was she kidding? He'd been barely out of high school, little more than a boy to her, a warrant officer doing her final NATO tour before she took early retirement, which had been offered because the military wanted to downsize.

Not that *she* was old. She just felt old compared to Rick, who was old enough to father her child and yet too young to drink in some provinces.

On an afterthought, she grabbed the tissue. With a mutter of thanks, she snatched the appointment card and strode out of the medical center, refusing to spare a glance at whoever sat patiently in the waiting room behind her, no doubt watching her fight her impending breakdown.

Rick Cahill. Young, bright, handsome. Eager without being naive, he'd been one of her best storesmen. He'd been a good driver, and a sensible soldier for his age.

And he knew his way around a woman's body.

The last duty she'd performed in Bosnia was to attend his memorial service.

Her eyes stung and her chest burned as she headed toward the drugstore across the street. *Think about prenatal vitamins, Sylvie. Nothing else.*

What would the other soldiers under her command have said if they'd known she and her youngest storesman had been together and that she'd sat in the front row of the chapel tent during his memorial service, carrying their dead friend's baby?

Thank heavens the military wanted to cut its forces. Thank heavens she'd escaped her unit before she discovered she was pregnant. She would have been repatriated immediately anyway, but the rumors would have whipped up like prairie dust.

She couldn't have looked them in the eye. Not after realizing the mistakes she'd made.

Not after signing the nondisclosure agreement.

Not after killing Rick.

Nausea surged into her throat at the thought of her cowardice. Clamping her hand over her mouth, she threw a wild look up the busy street. She had to make it back across to her car—and fast—if she was to vomit behind it.

Panic seized her. Would she make it? Standing on the curb, holding back bile, she spotted the receptionist from the medical center lead a man out into the brilliant sunshine. The woman scanned the street until her gaze settled on Sylvie. Touching the man's arm, the receptionist pointed directly at her.

Oh, boy. She wouldn't make it now. That guy, whoever he was, would intercept her. He was heading straight into disaster—

Striding across the street like he owned the town, the tall man fixed his stare on her. Rooted her to the sidewalk.

Within seconds he reached her. "Warrant Officer Mitchell?"

She stiffened, thankful the six-inch curb brought her eye level with him. "I'm retired now," she said after a bitter swallow. "Call me Sylvie."

"Sylvie?" The man tested the name on his tongue, all the while his riveting gaze drilling into her. "Sylvie."

Good heavens. The way he said her name conjured up warm, moonless nights when crickets provided the music...and someone in the dark provided the silky caresses.

Her bones melted. Were these hormones going to plague her like this for the next six months? Nauseated one minute, aroused the next?

She forced her voice to stay brisk. "What can I do for you?"

He studied her with eyes squinting against the sun. An incredible, body-weakening image of the fantasy from a moment ago wafted in on the warm southerly wind, as vivid as any nightmare her time in Bosnia still produced on those damned sleepless nights she'd had lately.

She didn't welcome either vision.

The man stepped onto the curb. Sylvie craned her neck to stare up at him. His ebony hair lifted with the breeze, the same breeze that delivered a warm, lingering male scent to her keen nose. She couldn't help but inhale it, draw it deeply in and hold it.

"Were you recently in Bosnia?" he asked.

Her jaw tightened and she wet her lips. "Yes." Most soldiers took Bosnia in stride, a tour of duty that was difficult but necessary.

She'd wished, mostly in the dead of night when the horror returned, that she had the same casual outlook.

The government believed the Former Yugoslavia had been stabilized. They wouldn't give credence to the small pocket of resistance she'd faced that night, a resistance she knew had friends inside her own camp.

Instead, NATO and the new Bosnian government had discounted those who'd ambushed her truck, diplomatically announcing that the group would eventually negotiate or disperse. No, they weren't associated with any terrorists. They'd see the light as soon as they realized their actions weren't getting the media's attention.

Sylvie couldn't manage the same simplistic view. Too many frightening, conflicting memories. Begging children and mined areas too dangerous to even graze goats, now overgrown with various self-seeded grains. Food for hungry children that was too risky to harvest.

And Rick, killed in an ambush she could never acknowledge because of that damn simplistic view…and a nondisclosure agreement.

The man cut deep into her thoughts with his smooth voice. "You had a young soldier working for you. A Rick Cahill?"

The sun beat hard on her back. With no breakfast to fortify her, her knees weakened to those of a newborn calf. And her everchurning stomach—

She swallowed again, at the same time locking her knees to steady them. "Yes, Rick worked for me." How did she manage to sound so calm?

The man's piercing eyes darkened and the creases between his brows deepened. "I'm Jon Cahill. Rick's brother. I've come to find out exactly what happened to Rick the night he died."

Jon waited for the woman in front of him to answer.

All she did was pale dramatically. If he hadn't seen an obvious faint before, he'd have accused Sylvie Mitchell of offering a distraction to hide something important concerning Rick's death.

He might still do that.

But her eyes glazed over and one undulating wave wobbled through her body. His wife, no, ex-wife now, had done this exact same damn thing before she'd dropped to the ground. She'd been pregnant with another man's child.

Jon caught Sylvie Mitchell before she fell. Quickly he wrapped his left arm around her back and bent to shove his right hand under her jean-clad knees. Scooping her up, he marched across the street and straight back into the medical center.

Thankfully, an elderly couple opened all the doors for him, and the startled receptionist who a moment before had pointed out Sylvie, hurried to locate a free bed in the adjoining ward.

"She's fainted," he stated, laying her down on the examination bed. A nurse bustled in, shoving him back as she began a quick assessment.

A movement caught his attention. The receptionist had opened the door to leave, but not before eyeing him with open curiosity. Did she expect him to follow?

No way. And he told her so with a sharp frown before she hurried out. Jon turned back to the examination table.

After checking Sylvie's vital signs, the nurse rolled her into the recovery position. Then she looked up at him. "What was she doing when she fainted?"

"Talking to me. I caught her before she fell."

"Good thing. She could have really rapped her head." She slung the stethoscope around her neck. "Her vitals are fine, but I'll get the doctor to look at her, just in case.'' She stalked over to the wide medicine cabinet and pulled out a clear capsule. She returned to the bed, broke it open and shoved it under Sylvie's nose.

Sylvie flinched. Her eyelids fluttered wide and she batted the nurse's hand away. ''Ew! What the hell?''

The nurse smiled as she discarded the smelling salts. ''Works every time.'' She peered down at Sylvie before patting her hand. ''You fainted. Lie still. I'll ask the doctor to check you over.''

The nurse left them alone. Jon remained by the window, again speculating on whether the faint had been a ploy to avoid answering his question. The military had pulled every other damn stunt to prevent him from learning exactly what had happened the night Rick died.

Like the night he'd called Rick's commanding officer. Oh, the man had been more than polite, calling Jon ''sir'' and showing in his voice the right amount of sympathy and concern. But Jon's gut tightened with intuition when the man turned vague about the details: investigation still on-going; bad weather that night; trouble finding the truck they'd sent out on detail.

Jon was a police officer in Canada's biggest city. Lies, omissions, and cover-ups came with the territory, and there were some of each crossing through the phone lines that night.

''Trouble finding the truck?'' he'd barked back. ''How could that happen? You sent them out on a detail, with a route to follow?''

''The weather was poor, Mr. Cahill,'' the commander had answered. ''I'm sorry, but the connection is bad on this end. I must tell you, we're still investigating your brother's death very thoroughly.''

''What did his supervisor say happened?''

"Warrant Officer Mitchell gave her statement that night, sir, and has already repatriated back to Canada."

Jon had frowned. "When?"

"The day after the memorial service, actually."

"Would it be possible to talk to her?"

"Mr. Cahill, I'm not at liberty to say any more—"

The line had gone dead, and Jon wagered it wasn't because of a bad connection. *Not at liberty to say.* The commander had been watching too many media interviews on TV.

Why had Rick's supervisor been shipped back so soon? She sure as hell got out of Dodge pretty damn quick. And why couldn't they find their own supply truck? Intuition burned hot inside of him.

Now the military would get a lesson in how good the police were with investigations. Finding Warrant Officer Sylvie Mitchell had been a breeze.

Jon focused on the woman lying in front of him, intuition still itching his skin. Something was definitely being covered up.

And Sylvie Mitchell was his last chance to find out what that was. God help her if she clammed up, as well. He walked over to the bed and leaned slightly forward. "Feeling better?"

Her eyes flew open, shock and horror flaring in them. And fear, too?

Fear of what? Him?

His anger dropped away like an icy stone. He wasn't here to scare the facts out of her. All he wanted was the truth about Rick, something he deserved above all else.

Sylvie Mitchell had better understand that.

Sylvie. The name conjured up the image of a sultry brunette with voluptuous curves and a come-hither smile.

This woman could only be the exact opposite. A blond,

she had lean, toned, minimal curves, and no way would he ever expect a beckoning, erotic smile to crack her efficient, porcelain complexion.

"As soon as you started to wobble, I picked you up and carried you over here."

She blinked around the room. "Where am I?"

He followed her gaze. Judging from the posters and the odd-looking pieces of monitoring equipment, he realized this place must be a birthing room of some kind. "In the maternity ward attached to the medical center, I presume. I haven't got a lot of experience in this area." Not wanting to dwell on that fact, he turned back to her. "How do you feel?"

Sylvie inhaled and sat up, swinging her legs over the edge of the examination table. "Better. Thank you."

He shoved out his hand to stop her from rising off the bed. She wore a short-sleeved T-shirt, leaving plenty of exposed skin to touch.

Warm, dry skin. And softer under his fingertips than he'd expected from a soldier.

He yanked back his hand. "Just the same, wait for the doctor. There has to be some reason you fainted."

She shot him a wary look. "I missed breakfast."

Jon glanced at his watch. "It's only ten o'clock. What time do you Albertans get up?"

"Early." She looked the other way. "I run a ranch just outside of town, so I don't sleep in."

Jon was ready to shove her back onto the table, should she try to stand. But she didn't. Rather, with a soft exhalation, she lay back down and shut her eyes.

That was it? Jon waited for more, for anything to stop him from staring at her lean form: her right knee bent; breasts that were still firm enough to curve upward; and a thin line of flat stomach that looked as though it needed warm, moist kisses—

He swung away from her. Hell, maybe he *should* leave. He'd acted on impulse coming here, and through all the hours traveling, he'd envisioned a different Sylvie Mitchell, a different set of answers and a much different reaction to her.

He shoved aside the attraction. No way would he leave. He was so close to finally hearing the truth he could taste it.

But Sylvie Mitchell looked so vulnerable lying there. He cleared his throat and looked over at her. "Um, do you want me to get you something to eat?"

"Do you want me to throw up on you?"

Her face was so deadpan Jon couldn't help but smile. Yet the pitiful grin fell away quickly. Oh, cripes, it had been so long since he smiled it hurt his cheeks. "Not really."

She said no more, only lay there, eyes shut again, totally ignoring him.

"Ms. Mitchell?"

She opened her eyes.

"You knew my brother, didn't you?"

She blinked. "You don't look like him."

Annoyed that she didn't answer his question directly, he worked his jaw. "He took after our mother. I favor our father." Both of whom were dead, he wanted to add.

"Rick was so blond," she added softly, studying his face with a tiny frown. "And you're the exact opposite." She raised her eyebrows. "You say you're Rick's brother, but frankly you don't look like him. How do I know you're telling me the truth? You could be a reporter snooping out a story, for all I know."

Was there a story to snoop out? he wanted to ask. Instead, and without a word, he yanked his wallet from his back pocket and flipped it open onto the narrow area of examination table between them. She lifted her head to peer down at it.

He knew what it said. Jonathan Andrew Cahill. Toronto Police Services.

She slumped back on the bed. Oh, mercy. A police officer in search of the truth about his murdered brother.

Could it get any worse?

"You're a cop?"

"Like our father, before a drug pusher ambushed him."

Ambushed? Sylvie rubbed her arms, hoping the sudden goose bumps would disappear. She didn't need to be an expert in psychology to know that telling Jon his only brother had died in nearly the same fashion wouldn't be a good thing. Not while this man still carried a frustrated anger so big that she could practically see it roosting on his shoulder like a gargoyle.

"I'm sorry. I remember Rick telling me about him."

"He was a good police officer. Then some bastard killed him. And two years later that bastard walked out of court a free man."

What could she say? His bitter tone resounded through the room, bouncing off the walls and bombarding her, over and over. *A free man. When his father lay dead.*

She silently prayed he'd suggest they meet someplace, at a future date....

Something she could prepare for—or maybe even avoid.

The man heaved a burdened sigh as he picked up his wallet to pocket it. "Look, to say the least, the military has been vague about Rick's death. I have yet to receive anything in writing. I spoke to Rick's—and your—commanding officer, and…'' He paused, quite distinctly, too, leaving the impression he was tailoring his words carefully. ''…all he said was Rick was on a detail with you. Delivering rations to an outpost. The accident occurred in the mountains. Right?''

She studied the ceiling. Delivering rations to an outpost that didn't exist. Driving around the wrong mountain. ''Yes.'' She couldn't look at him and focus on his words at the same time. ''I'm sorry Rick died. He was a good soldier.''

Frustration surged inside of him. Damn it, that was it? A short apology for losing a good soldier? He hadn't come halfway across the country to hear that trite compliment. He hadn't been told by the chief of police to take all the time he needed to deal with Rick's death— even if it took all summer—just to hear what a good soldier Rick had been.

And he wouldn't ignore the suspicion gripping his gut at her brush-off. No blasted way.

His mouth thinned. ''Rick was a hell of a lot more than just a good soldier.''

He watched her blink, fear in the gaze she suddenly couldn't level on him. Fear again? It had to be something else.

''You were with him when he died, weren't you?''

She said nothing. Jon crushed the urge to grab her and shake her and demand the whole damn, blasted truth once and for all. But, checking his fury, he clenched his fists and stalked to the window.

Finally she spoke, her voice so barely above a whisper he had to hold his breath to hear her. ''I'm so sorry. We'd driven—'' She checked her words, for what reason, he couldn't guess. ''We'd done similar details before. Got stuck together overnight more often than not because of mudslides or bad weather. Never once had we been ambushed.''

He whirled, his heart pounding, his throat suddenly dry. It took him a minute to find his voice. ''Ambushed? No one said anything about an ambush! What the hell are you talking about?''

Horrified, she fell silent again and looked away.

Ambush? Was that what the military was keeping from him? Rick had been attacked, in a country purporting to be at peace.

No. Even ambushes make the news, especially in these troubled times.

He stalked over to her and pressed a fist on either side of the black vinyl table, not caring if he towered over her like a madman. ''I want to know about this ambush. *Now.*''

She wouldn't even look at him. Swearing internally, he pulled back and raked his fingers through his hair. So close to the truth! So close he could feel it teasing him. How could she shut up now? ''Look, Ms. Mitchell. Sylvie. My only living relative has died and no one will give me any details. Do you think that's fair? Do you think Rick deserves to be forgotten so easily?'' He sucked in a long breath in a desperate attempt to control his growing frustration.

Her hand strayed to her belly. The sunlight streaming in the window behind him caught a narrow, glimmering trail of a tear as it escaped her eye. She furtively swiped it away and pushed herself up, this time meeting his glare with equal intensity. ''Rick isn't forgotten, all right? I was there. I tried to keep him alive, but I couldn't.'' She paled, then sagged. Was she going to pass out again? ''Now, could you please leave me alone?''

The door swung open and in strolled the doctor. He carried a clipboard and smiled at Sylvie. "Good morning. I hear you've fainted."

Jon glanced at Sylvie. She lay back down and closed her eyes. "Yes, I did."

The doctor directed his attention to Jon. "Could you please leave us for a few minutes? I won't be long."

Jon looked to Sylvie, hoping that somehow she might ask him to stay. But of course she wouldn't. They were strangers, regardless of the fact she'd been with his only relative up until the moment—

Unable to form the words in his mind, Jon stormed out of the room. He might as well write off talking to Sylvie Mitchell today. But she'd mentioned a ranch outside of town. It wouldn't be hard to find, despite there being nearly as many ranches here as Stetsons. Maybe talking on her own turf would make her feel less intimidated. And, hopefully, she'd have eaten by then and couldn't use the excuse of fainting to avoid conversation.

For a tall, strong woman, she didn't look the type to faint for lack of food. In fact, she looked pretty damn good, period. When he'd spotted her across the street, her creamy complexion had looked healthy, her body toned. Her short, blond hair gleamed with good health.

Her skin soft like warm peaches against his.

Whoa, Cahill. That's pushing it, don't you think?

Suspicion still curdling inside of him, Jon stalked down the corridor to the receptionist's desk. He'd ask for a phone book there. He'd find her ranch.

"Excuse me?"

He turned at the sound of the voice. The receptionist bustled past him and behind the counter, throwing a smile at him as she went. "Don't worry about her. She'll be

fine. Soon she'll be outside, enjoying this lovely day.
Best way to start the summer, isn't it, with a great weekend ahead, weatherwise. Do you have her medical insurance card? I'll need it.''

He bristled at the bright, cheery chatter. It had been a
long time since he'd been in a small town. Toronto
wasn't the kind of place where people struck up friendly
conversations with perfect strangers. They barely made
eye contact. And being a cop, he found himself suspicious whenever someone he didn't know started talking.

But he wouldn't ignore the opportunity. ''I'm sorry. I
don't have her card. I'm still worried about her,'' he said,
hedging his way into the conversation. ''She's…not the
kind to faint.''

''It happens like this sometimes, but the symptoms
should pass soon. You must be a…'friend' of hers?'' Her
stare was openly curious. She stood there, no doubt hoping he would fill the empty silence with an answer.

He forced a brief smile onto his face. Now why should
she put so much emphasis on the word *friend?* He gave
her a knowing look. ''More than a friend, believe me.''
Perhaps this chatty little receptionist could direct him out
to Sylvie's ranch?

The woman smiled back. Abruptly, the doctor strolled
behind the counter and dropped a slim file on the desk
along with a few sample packs of medicine from his
pocket.

Jon glanced at them as they fell onto the file. Prenatal
vitamins, in pale-pink wrappers.

Prenatal?

''Give these to Ms. Mitchell, will you, Fleur? And I
want to see her in my office first thing next Wednesday
morning.'' The doctor noticed Jon, and his smile broad-

ened. "Your wife's fine. Though I suggest you take her home and feed her. She shouldn't miss any more meals."

Jon nodded, unwilling to correct the man on their marital status. The mistake could prove useful. "I will."

The doctor gone, the receptionist scooped up the vitamins and smiled at him. "See? Nothing that won't cure itself by December."

His face fell. Talk about hitting the jackpot. All he'd hoped for were directions to her ranch.

Fainting, prenatal vitamins. The look of horror on her face when he spoke of Rick. The hand that slid to her flat belly.

Stuck overnight more often than not, she'd said.

Taking the offered vitamin samples, he strode down the hall. The cure coming in December? A hasty bit of mental math quickened his step. He should have known. Hadn't his ex-wife fainted that one day and blamed it on missing a meal? Right before asking for a divorce? She'd been queasy all through their meetings with the lawyers. A blessing that had ended in an uncontested divorce.

She'd practically raced out to her lover after that, leaving him at the lawyer's office with a bitter taste in his mouth.

A mental litany of the secrets she'd kept from him danced in his mind. The path ahead of him was starting to look pretty damn familiar, and while Tanya's secrets meant squat to him now, Sylvie Mitchell's were worth a hell of a lot more.

Jon thinned his lips. Did this have something to do with Rick's commanding officer's reluctance to speak to him?

His heart pounded in his throat as he swung open the door to the labor room. Damn appropriate room, he'd say.

Sylvie looked up as he strode in.

"Feeling better now?" His tight voice sliced the quiet. A tiny frown creased her forehead. "Fine, thank you."

He gritted his teeth as he dropped the pink packages into her lap. "So, is it Rick's baby you're carrying, or did you two just talk on those nights you were stuck together?"

Chapter 2

After spending thirteen years in army logistics and supply, Sylvie had met her share of intimidating jerks. Most she either ignored or answered with a blunt, uncomplainable "Yes, sir."

But cornered in this stifling birthing room, she could do neither. Nor was it in her nature to lie. She had kept herself as honest as possible in a trade that had more thieving bin rats than it had army boots.

Try as she might, she couldn't ignore the intimidating man who filled the doorway, any more than she could have ignored him when he scooped her up like a child and walked calmly across the street to the clinic.

Oh, she hadn't been so fully unconscious that she didn't realize she was being carried. She'd felt his arms around her, the heat of his chest penetrating deep into her...and, well, if truth were told, she hadn't minded it one bit.

They say one's whole value system changes when one

faints; it certainly had with her. But not to the point of telling this man she was carrying his nephew or niece. What if he asked more questions? What if he wanted to know how serious she'd been with Rick? What if he learned the truth?

She turned her attention to the window, wishing it could open and let in the strong mountain breeze she so desperately needed. "What did the receptionist tell you?"

"Nothing you could use in a formal complaint, if that's what you're thinking. I put two and two together. I'm right, aren't I? You're pregnant."

If she opened her mouth, she'd tell the truth, the way she'd always done. She pursed her lips.

Jon continued, his arms folded over his chest. "I'll take that as a yes. I didn't know you and Rick were so close. He always spoke highly of you, but in a supervisor-subordinate sense. Or so I understood."

She slid off the bed, ignoring the sharp pang of hunger that booted away her fading nausea. "Look, yes, I'm pregnant, okay? But as to who the father is, that's my business, not yours."

She tried to brush past him, but he stepped in front of the door and at the same time kicked it shut with the heel of his shoe.

The sharp click echoed around the hot, quiet room.

"We're not done talking, Ms. Mitchell."

Her head shot up. For the first time, she stared hard at him, forcing herself to notice every little detail of his handsome face.

She'd like nothing better than to fire back that he had no right to decide when she was done talking. She leaned in close....

Too close and way too personal for her liking.

Well, maybe not totally against her liking. If circumstances had been different…

His coal-black hair wasn't neat the way his smooth polo shirt and pressed pants were. Maybe he was the kind of man who ran his fingers constantly through it.

She peered into his narrowed eyes, recognizing in the dark, brittle-blue irises a hint of Rick. Although Rick's would have narrowed in the sunlight only, not out of mistrust like this man. She'd rarely seen Rick without one of his trademark, handsome grins. He had trusted so easily, she thought, her stomach tightening again.

Shaken by the memories she'd conjured up, she stepped back from Jon.

Somewhere from down the corridor, a baby wailed. Jon snapped his head around, listening. The crying stopped almost immediately.

Out of the corner of his eye, he looked at her. "I wonder if it was the father or the mother who picked that baby up. What do you think?"

"I'm sure it was the nurse." She took another step forward again. "Now, please excuse me, Mr. Cahill."

"Call me Jon. Because you're going to see a lot of me in the future," he said in a smooth-as-silk voice.

She shot a sharp glare into his calm features. "I haven't confirmed your suspicions, Mr. Cahill."

"It's my business to read people's faces, Sylvie. Yours is no different. I'm not condemning you for carrying my brother's child. I'm just telling you I *will* be a part of its life."

"You didn't tell me how you came to suspect such a thing."

"The receptionist gave me a date when you'll be 'cured,' and from your commanding officer, I learned when you left Bosnia. You retired eleven weeks ago immediately after Rick's memorial service. You've been pregnant about twelve weeks, haven't you?''

What could she say? She nodded.

"You told me you and Rick got stuck overnight more often than not, confirming what Rick had already told me in his e-mails.'' He drew in a deep breath, as if controlling some troubling part of himself. "Rick died March twenty-sixth. All of these facts plus the way you reacted when I mentioned him made me suspicious. Am I correct?''

Hunger kicked at her again, but this time she fought off the pangs. She could stand on a parade square for days, shifting very little, never feeling hungry, tired or woozy. Yet today, feeling like the stuff at the bottom of a horse stall, she could barely nod her head.

She managed to anyway. What was the use? It didn't take a rocket scientist to know that this guy…with eyes like frozen diamonds, who had cradled her in a way she hadn't figured she would want to be cradled…he wouldn't give up until he knew the truth.

"Yes," she whispered, shocked that she was relenting. "This is Rick's baby."

Wait. She'd plowed through a tour of duty in one of the world's worst war zones without ever weakening, and yet one moment of Jon's questioning and she'd caved. What was wrong with her?

For starters, she *hadn't* plowed through the whole tour of duty without weakening. There was that one night…when she'd thought only of herself. And how she hadn't wanted to die a—

Jon folded his strong-looking arms across his powerful chest and nodded. Sylvie's knees wobbled, and she recalled briefly how good it had felt being carried, her head sagging against his firm, warm shoulder.

"Good." Leaning forward, he took her arm and steered her into the corridor without so much as looking her way. "Now that we have that confirmation out of the way, I'll drive you home. On the way, you can tell me what everyone said about the age difference between you and Rick. It must be more than ten years."

Jonathan Cahill was a bastard. And Sylvie knew bastards. They came a dime a dozen in the army. This man cut to the quick, wasted no words and had a damn annoying expectation that his questions would be answered truthfully and immediately.

And he scared her. Rick had told her once that his parents were both dead, leaving him and his brother alone. What he had neglected to tell her was that his older brother was as possessive of Rick's memory as he was downright nasty.

She would have protested the way he directed her out of the medical center, but she didn't want to call attention to herself, or her condition.

The hot Albertan sun beat down on her when they stepped outside. How she managed to reach Jon's rental car was beyond her. Of course, his firm grip on her elbow had helped.

No! She didn't need his help. She shrugged off his hand and with a deep breath, managed to stay upright as Jon unlocked the car with the touch of a remote control. She took the opportunity of his averted attention to recover her faltering independence. If he had thought of helping her inside, he was mistaken. She threw open the door and climbed in.

Oh, my. Leather seats. Cool, smooth, yielding to her hot, aching form like the surf on the Adriatic beach where she'd taken her four-day R&R, back in November.

Jon Cahill had rented the best car in town.

She sank against the backrest.

"Good thing I parked in the shade," he said, climbing in beside her and starting the engine. He glanced up at one of the large red maples that lined the parking lot. "It would be hot enough to have you faint again."

She didn't comment as he cranked up the air-conditioning.

"Which way?" he asked.

She directed him out of town, uncertainty nibbling at her. She couldn't imagine the military divulging its secrets, and she doubted that Jon had come all this way to merely find closure. He knew more. Or he suspected more.

He'd said something about not knowing the truth. During the debrief, her CO had told her the military still had to finish their investigation. Considering what she knew, yes, of course, she was expected to keep silent. And for once Sylvie had been in full agreement. She had no desire to discuss what had really happened, especially with Jon Cahill and his obvious deep-seated bitterness.

She cleared her throat. "I'm sorry about your father. My mother died about ten years ago."

"So you live with your dad on your ranch?"

"Now that I've taken over the place, yes. Sort of. I did when I came home on leave, of course." She sighed at her foolish stumble of words. "I guess I do now. But he and Andrea go south in the winter. A few years ago he remarried. My stepmother…she's great and all, but…"

"But what?"

Sylvie shrugged. "I don't know her very well. She's a lot younger than Dad and loves the great outdoors. They take university students on primitive expeditions all summer long. They've been gone for the past two weeks."

"I see."

Great. She sounded like a jealous daughter, but she wasn't. Andrea kept Dad active and alive. She was good for him and had even convinced her father to sign the ranch over to Sylvie, something Sylvie had secretly hoped would happen.

"So you haven't told your father about your pregnancy yet. And you don't know how to, either, right?"

"Reading my face again?"

"Among other things." He turned to her when they stopped at Trail's only traffic light, and as they lingered at the intersection, his gaze drifted up from her knees, pausing at her hips a moment, before completing the inspection with a journey to her face. "How long will your father be gone?"

"Most of the summer. On and off. And I'm not worried about what he'll say. Dad is, well, mildly supportive of everything I do. Andrea might want to help a bit too much, but at least she's never had a baby, so I won't get too much anecdotal advice."

He kept staring at her face, as if gauging whether or not she was telling him the truth. Then, as if he'd just remembered he was driving, he noticed the green light and eased the sports car into the intersection.

"What about your mother? Tell me about her," she asked. He blinked once before answering.

"She died a few years ago."

Yes, of course. Now she remembered. Rick had told her that lung cancer from too many cigarettes had killed his mother.

"You don't smoke, I hope," Jon said, as if reading her thoughts yet again.

"No."

"Good."

The traffic lessened as they put the town behind them and brought the foothills closer. Sylvie forced herself to relax, but the effort was in vain. The man beside her radiated the tension of a coiled spring. One sudden shift of the unknown force that held him together, and that spring would fly out like a destructive missile.

Ridiculous idea. He was a grieving man, not a loose cannon. Besides, she could handle loose cannons if she had to. She'd taken leadership courses. She knew—and had practiced—all the styles of leadership. She'd been good at soldiering.

Leaders were made, not born, the military touted, and she'd always believed that. But this man? He would have aced any of those courses. Leadership seemed as sculpted to him as the smooth, tanned skin he wore.

"Turn right here," she told him, glad she could occupy them both with her directions. Because as soon as they reached her ranch, she'd offer her thanks, her condolences and then ask him to leave.

Jon turned the car when Sylvie pointed to a sign at the start of a long driveway. "Mountainview Ranch Campgrounds," he read out loud. He didn't understand. "A campground? I thought you said this was a ranch?"

"It was. And still is. When ranching bottomed out a few years ago, my father cut way back on the number of cattle and decided to diversify. A campground was one of the ideas he came up with. You know, campers wanting to experience ranch life the easy way, with motor homes and wagon rides?"

Jon peered out the side window to his left, noticing the small barn and corral that filled the center of the circular driveway. "And he's raising exotic animals, too?"

Sylvie let out a short laugh. "Andrea's contribution was a small petting zoo for the kids. She had to justify bringing a pot-bellied pig into their marriage. Since then, we've acquired a mule deer, two llamas and six foul-tempered Canada Geese who never want to fly south in the fall. But the kids love them."

Jon touched the brakes when he spied a small group of children, who, ignoring the sign not to feed the animals, chucked handfuls of grass over the fence to the llamas.

"You can't work this ranch alone. You've just retired, and now you're expecting," he stated the obvious.

"I have some hands. Lawrence is my biggest help, and I had three others, though one quit in the spring. They're all expected to work both the campground and the ranch."

"Big ranch?" In one easy sweep, he assessed the house where his nephew or niece would call home. Not a bad location. What kid wouldn't love a ranch-cum-campground with zoo animals and wide-open spaces? He and Rick had spent their childhood in a postage-stamp-size home in middle-class Toronto.

"Not like it used to be. Only forty-two breeding cows on less than 100 acres, twenty of which are now used for camping."

"Not much to graze on."

"No, it isn't. We grow some silage, but thankfully, because we're small, we're entitled to lease a certain portion of federal land. It works out well for us, the government land being el-shaped and connected to our land by a good trail. I used to ride out there all the time."

"A lot of work?"

She shrugged, trying to make it appear everything was fine. She failed. And he knew it. It was a hell of a lot more work than she was making it out to be. "We manage okay. Most of the work's in the late fall, anyway."

Jon drove up to the main house, following Sylvie's directions, his eyes focusing on the sprawling bungalow. The house was set apart from the campground office, which sat over to his right. He eased to a stop just as Sylvie threw open her door.

"Thanks for the ride. I feel better already."

He snapped his attention back to her, scrambling out of the car before she could bolt into the house. "How are you going to get your car back?"

She stopped at his front bumper. "I'll send the men in later. It's no big deal. We make trips into town all the time." After a pause she added, "Like I said, thanks for the lift."

"That's it?" Jeez, she couldn't just expect to cut him loose. "Just thanks?" He clenched his jaw to check his rising temper. "I came here to find out what happened the night Rick died. No one will tell me. Even the death certificate didn't say one damn thing. Just 'death as a result of an accident.' No one's at liberty to say. I even had to wait to bury him, and I'll be damned if I'm waiting any longer to find out how he died."

Her face impassive, Sylvie stared at him while he vented his fury. He took another seething breath and added, "Put yourself in my shoes. After all of that, I find out my brother's warrant officer is carrying his baby, and you want me to walk away with just a 'thanks for the lift'?"

He tightened his fingers into painful fists, trying to force his body to stop shaking. When it refused, he stalked up close to Sylvie. Only when she stepped back in an attempt to retake her comfort zone, did he realize how far he was willing to push the issue.

He'd push it all the way, if he had to. He would stay here as long as it took to find out the truth. Hadn't his chief suggested as much?

He looked down at Sylvie's face. So clear, with features so fine and smooth it was hard to believe she'd made a career in the army. "How did my brother die? How long had you two been intimate? Was this baby planned between you two? Or did it just happen? Were you planning to marry?"

She went white. Cursing, he grabbed her arm and steered her past the wild tangle of weeds and up the crooked steps of her verandah. Damn, he should have waited before he lost his cool. But she seemed as likely to brush him off as her commanding officer had, as the escort officer had when Jon had driven up to Ottawa to meet the Hercules aircraft that had carried Rick's remains back to Canada. That man informed him that an autopsy had been scheduled. Jon had even had to wait to bury him. To grieve properly.

At the front door he steeled himself, wondering briefly if he should push himself into her home. "Let's get you inside. I'll find you something to eat, all right?"

She jerked her arm back, her eyes wary yet unwilling to meet his. "I'm fine. Look, I'm sorry Rick died. I really am. Good grief, I'm carrying his baby. I wish I could, but I can't tell you anything about his death. I signed a nondisclosure agreement, and the investigation—"

With a frown and lips that snapped shut, she stopped. He waited, silently urging her on. "That's all I can say," she added.

Too hurriedly, he thought.

She shook her head, finally blurting out, "Bosnia isn't

a placid little country, as much as the Bosnian government wants it to be. It's a war zone, Jon. Soldiers die in
war zones. Rick died in the line of duty. You should try
to find some comfort in that.''

"Do you?"

She pulled away from him and stalked into the house.
The door would have slammed shut in his face had he
not been close enough behind her to throw out his palm
and deflect it.

He followed her down the quiet hallway. When they
reached the kitchen, Sylvie stopped and Jon nearly ran
into her. His own gaze trailed after hers as she looked
across the kitchen table to an older man, who stood holding a coffee cup.

"Dad?" she said, obviously surprised. "What are you
doing home?"

Sylvie tried to smile at her father, to return the warmth
in the grin he offered, but her hunger and Jon plowing
into the kitchen behind her weakened her feeble attempt.

She watched her father's gaze linger on her face a
moment, then snap to Jon. She cleared her throat. "Dad,
this is Jon Cahill. His brother was Rick Cahill. Remember, the…one who died?''

She needed to say more to her father. But now? She
couldn't just blurt out that she was also pregnant with
Rick's baby and that Jon Cahill had driven her home
because she'd fainted on Trail's main street.

No. Dad deserved to be told in a more private setting
that he was going to be a grandfather.

How would he react? Sometimes, when she was
young, he peered down at her after a long day outside,
with a tired look that seemed to ask who she was. There

was always something more important to do than to listen to his daughter's endless, excitable chatter.

Old news, she told herself. Dad's happy now.

She looked at Jon. "This is my father, Allister Mitchell." She bustled past them as they shook hands across the table, not wanting to elaborate on why Jon was here, or why he'd stormed into the house after her. But she couldn't let Jon tell her father, especially in the no-nonsense terms in which he seemed to express himself.

"Jon came to Trail looking for me. He wanted to discuss what happened to Rick."

Allister nodded. When she first arrived home, Sylvie had given him and Andrea the briefest of explanations. Rick and she had been driving to one of the outposts when a slide had stopped them. Rick had been injured and unfortunately he'd died.

She swallowed. No thanks to her.

Her father had the wisdom to let it go at that, and Sylvie was thankful the military had shut up on the details. After reporting on the death and the memorial service, the media had turned its focus on the other hot spots around the world.

"So, Jon," her father was saying, "how did you find Sylvie? She doesn't go into town regularly." He turned to her. "Why *did* you go in? Lawrence noticed you didn't take the truck, so it wouldn't have been for supplies."

Lawrence was their old ranch hand. A second father to her. She straightened her shoulders and smiled at Allister. Without Andrea at his side, her father seemed much more approachable. Andrea would fuss too much and take over the whole conversation.

She drew in a deep breath. Delaying the inevitable had never been her way. She'd already delayed acknowledging her pregnancy longer than she should have. Besides, if Jon wanted to be part of her baby's life, then he may as well see his whole, "newly acquired family" in a clear, transparent light, warts and all. She had no idea what her father would say, and a part of her hoped, for Jon's sake, that her father would show some of that blunt Mitchell candor that Andrea seemed to have smoothed out so effectively.

She stared at her father, steeled her shoulders and said, "Dad, I'm pregnant. I went in to make a doctor's appointment."

Allister's face went blank. "Pregnant? Who's the father? It can't be him—" He pointed to Jon. "You only just met, didn't you?"

With a sigh and a stifled smile, Sylvie shook her head and threw open the refrigerator door. "No, it's not him." She realized how foolish she'd been, blurting out her condition. She had no desire to discuss the circumstances of the conception with anyone, especially with Jon avidly eavesdropping. "It happened in Bosnia. I'll tell you all about it later. We've got lots of time for that. Now, why are you here?"

Disoriented for a minute, he took his time answering, "One of the campers got ill. We carried him down on one of the pack horses, till we met the ambulance at the edge of the highway. Oh, he's going to be fine, just some bug. Andrea stayed up at the site with the rest of them. I was planning to go straight back out, but…"

She caught his speculative stare. "Go! There's not much to say, at least until I get my first doctor's appointment. I'm fine."

"You look like death warmed over, girl." He shook his head and turned to Jon. "Did you bring her home?"

Jon nodded. "As a matter of fact, I did. Personally, I

don't think she can do too much around here. You may want to stay back.''

She slammed the refrigerator shut. ''Wait a minute! I said I'm fine. There's nothing you can do, Dad, so there's no reason why you shouldn't go straight back up to Andrea. I have Lawrence—''

Allister let out a snort. ''Oh, Lawrence is busy enough with the campground. And he's getting too old. Plus, we lost Tyler last month. He was supposed to help you. Can you haul around fence posts and fix up the house by yourself in your condition?''

Oh, dear. She knew where this conversation was heading, and quickly shook her head. ''Of course I can't, but—''

''No, she can't,'' Jon announced. ''But I can.''

Sylvie snatched the swear word before it flew from her lips. Instead she glared at him. ''You have another job, remember? You're a cop in Toronto.''

A hint of regret whisked over his features. Regret? Fear? It had happened so fast, she couldn't be sure.

''A cop?'' her father interjected, making Sylvie wish she'd kept her mouth shut and made him think Jon was nothing but a bum off the street. Yeah, in a fine-looking polo shirt and pants that still bore an arrow-sharp crease. Allister Mitchell lived in his own world, but he wasn't naive. She could no more make Jon Cahill look like a disreputable drifter than she could undo the horror of this past spring.

''I can easily get the summer off,'' Jon said. ''There are plenty of auxiliary officers looking for extra hours. Remember what I said, back there in the clinic, don't you?''

The air, warmed by the sun streaming in the window above the sink, stuck hard in her throat. She could read so very easily the warning in Jon's expression. He *will* be a part of her baby's life. *Get used to it,* his eyes added.

But also, a suggestion of what he'd *not* said seemed to linger in the air. Who the father of her baby was.

Time stalled. Was he going to tell her father? She wished, however briefly, she'd told him the truth back there in the clinic. Every last detail that would have seen him storming out of Trail and straight to a good lawyer. The military could use a good lawsuit for all they'd done to Rick. Unless Jon chose to sue her, instead.

Sylvie tore her gaze from Jon, catching her father's raised eyebrows and questioning smile.

"What do you think, Sylvie? It's your ranch, now. If he can do the work, there's no reason why we can't hire him for the summer."

There were a thousand reasons why they shouldn't hire Jon Cahill. He wanted the truth from her about Rick, the details of Rick's last hours, not a sterilized military version.

All those shameful details.

And he wanted to be a part of her baby's life.

No. This baby was hers, not his. She would give it life, love it and raise it all by herself. She'd managed a career in the military by herself, and she'd managed to grow up without her father being around when she needed him. She would manage her new career as mother equally fine.

Without Jon Cahill, thank you very much.

"Well, Sylvie?" her father prompted.

Sylvie dared another look at Jon, half-afraid his intensity and tenacity might snare her. Those blue eyes seemed stronger, reflecting the determination he practically exuded from every pore on his strong body.

"Do I have the job, Sylvie?" As if purposely designed

to contrast his powerful stare, his tone turned quiet, persuasive.

There was that silky version of her name, too.

This was insane. But to protest too much would be akin to suicide. Jon Cahill's suspicions would soar through the roof if she kept refusing to hire him when she so obviously needed help.

"All right," she found herself saying. He wanted the job, well, he could have it. She'd keep him so busy this summer, he'd ache to return to the easy life in Toronto. And every night when his head hit his pillow—out in the bunkhouse with the rest of the men—he'd be out like a light, forgetting, or regretting, that he'd ever told her he wanted to be a part of his brother's child's life.

A smile grew slowly on his face. It wasn't much, but it did reach his eyes.

Her skin warmed and tingled in a subtle primitive answer, and those damn horrid hormones prickled under her skin again. For one stunning moment he did look just like Rick.

What had she got herself into? One night of fear and she'd broken her cardinal rule of never getting involved with another soldier.

She'd admired Rick, liked him, and had wanted him to excel in his career. But she hadn't wanted an intimate relationship with him.

So why did you? Because of that you got him killed. The words arced across her brain, firing up another horrible wash of memories.

"Excellent."

Mercifully, Jon's words cut through her thoughts, and she blinked up at him. The smile, however, had slid from his eyes, leaving only cool, smug resolve.

He'd won, and he knew it, the bastard. He indicated the chair in front of her father. ''Let's get you something to eat. Then while you're showing me what to do, you can tell me all about Rick.''

Chapter 3

"So, where are you staying?" Sylvie asked Jon before biting into the sandwich she'd thrown together. Her father had headed back out to Andrea and all the primitive campers. She'd given him a brief kiss and short hug, complete with a reassuring smile. Then she'd practically dived into the refrigerator.

Expressionless, Jon answered her question. "I'm not staying anywhere. As soon as I pulled into town, I headed into the nearest building to see if I could find out where you lived."

Her stomach settling and accepting food now, Sylvie swallowed her bite. "Which was the medical center, right? How convenient I should have just left there."

He lifted his eyebrows. "It's the first thing you see when you enter town. And it's big enough to service the whole community. I took a gamble that you might have gone there to find a doctor for yourself when you retired."

She took another hearty bite of her sandwich. He was right about her needing a doctor. Being in the military had meant all her medical needs had been taken care of. "Good guess."

Jon took the pitcher of milk and poured a large glass for her. "I never guess. I study people and use common sense."

She grimaced at the milk. "Then you should be fully aware how I feel about people pampering me. I can pour my own milk, thank you."

One corner of his mouth lifted up. "No need to get in a snit. I'm just being polite. I was hoping to get a cold drink, too."

"Help yourself." With one finger, she shoved the untouched glass toward him. "I guess now that you're working here, you're expecting to stay in the bunkhouse. Right?"

He shoved her glass of milk back in front of her. After helping himself to one of the glasses drying on the rack by the sink, he poured himself the rest of the milk. "Absolutely. Does that pose a problem for you?"

"What if I said the bunkhouse was full?"

"I'd buy a tent and stay at the campground."

Of course he would. "I've told you all I can about Rick. So what do you hope to achieve here? It's not to earn any extra money. Your job in Toronto must pay five times what I can pay you."

"I told you I want to be a part of Rick's baby's life. But you don't want me around. If I work here all summer, maybe I can convince you I'm sincere."

She laughed, despite herself. "I knew that much. I can see you're sincere at everything you do."

He didn't share her laugh. Which was just as well. Her

sarcasm hadn't meant to be one of those cute, tension-breaking quips.

He drained his milk. "Sylvie, your baby needs a father in its life. Its own father is dead, your father could do the job, but a child needs more than a grandfather who likes to camp and is ready to retire with his younger wife. I want the chance to prove to you I can be that father figure for your baby."

She gaped at him. A father? The idea of a cozy trio bombarded her, smashing the comfortable discussion. She swallowed down her latest bite. Jon, a father to her child? He didn't have a clue what he was saying, or the extent of what had happened to bring him here. He wouldn't be offering if he did. "How are you going to do that? You're the uncle who lives in Toronto. And what makes you think I can't provide a father figure for this baby?"

His eyes narrowed. "How, by scouring the high school for another kid Rick's age?"

She shoved back her chair and stood. "You're talking yourself out of a job, Cahill." She swung away from him, snatching her plate as she went. Only when she'd reached the sink and had fired the plate into it, did she count to ten.

Every swear word she'd ever learned rose in her, but she continued counting. Eight, nine…

"I'm sorry." Jon walked around the table and stopped beside her at the sink.

She looked at him, battling the fury roiling inside her.

"I was out of line."

She swung around to find him frowning at her. When he turned his attention to the vista seen from her kitchen window, she grabbed an opportunity to study his profile.

A straight, strong nose centered his even features. Rick

had that same handsome profile, but his face hadn't had the age and life experience to season it, as Jon's had.

Good grief, Rick had been so young. For a second she could so clearly picture him, right where Jon now stood, his whole body focused on his task as he drove through the wet snow and mud....

Moments before they slammed into the landslide that had been deliberately set.

An hour or so before they'd done the unthinkable. A few hours before he'd died.

Before she'd gotten him killed, just to satisfy a selfish, ludicrous desire.

Sylvie swallowed the hard lump in her throat and fought off another stinging round of shameful memories. From the moment they scrambled into the back of the truck, to await the Quick Reaction Force, the truth and the official report diverged widely.

She would never bridge them, either.

Jon turned to face her once more. Mercifully, Rick disappeared from her mind as she watched Jon's eyes moisten and cloud over. "Sylvie, I'm really sorry. I should never have said that crap about high school. You and Rick must have cared for each other. A lot, if you're carrying his baby. And to watch him die...." His voice faded into a hoarse whisper. "You two were lovers. I'm only the brother."

Something clamped hard around her heart. She wanted nothing more than to corral the ache and the shame and all the guilty memories that dogged her every minute. She clenched her jaw, fighting the mix that wouldn't be corralled.

Seeing the torment, Jon swore and hauled her into his arms. She went stiff, taken aback by his sudden compassion, but he did not relent. He pulled her tighter still, pressing her head into the side of his neck, as he drove his hands and face into her short, unruly hair.

She could smell the faded scent of his soap. He'd missed a spot when he'd shaved that morning and it scraped her temple. For one instant Jon Cahill was human, suffering like her. She'd known him for two hours and already unwanted empathy forced her arms to wrap around him.

She tried her best to comfort him. He tightened his grip on her further, and strangely the embrace eased the aching within her instead.

"Thank you," he said into her hair. "Thank you for giving me this chance."

For the next few minutes they did nothing but hold each other. Every part of his front touched her. He'd managed to shift his feet to enclose hers, and from his ankles up, his body fed hers with comfort. The whole long, firm length of him.

She sighed. Too soon to be offering such personal comfort, a part of her warned. He pulled back, only enough to see her face. She lifted her head, expecting to see tears still welling inside of his eyes.

But the look wasn't angry or grieving or anything she'd expected. Her heart reacted first, tripping up into a higher gear, as though it knew exactly what the look on his face meant before she even understood it herself.

His eyes, already dark in color, deepened, heating and stirring embers inside of her that should be left to grow cold. They'd sparked to life once, and look where she now found herself?

Jon's gaze dropped to her parted lips, and then back up, slowly roaming her face, as if in search of something.

Then, with smooth precision, Jon lowered his head. He

was going to kiss her. And she *wanted* to feel those smooth, firm lips on hers.

Panic burst inside of her. He didn't want to kiss her. He couldn't. They shouldn't. He wasn't thinking about it. Was he?

As if arcing across to him, the panic flared in his own eyes. He pushed her away, driving his fingers into his hair, looking around the kitchen at everything except her.

He cleared his throat. "Why don't you show me what you want me to do? You can ask this Lawrence guy to show me the bunkhouse later, okay?"

He'd nearly kissed her! What the hell was he thinking of?

He wasn't sure if he even liked her, for Pete's sake. She was far from the woman he'd mentally pictured Rick would end up with. On the exterior, Sylvie seemed like most single women in positions of authority.

But there was also a part of her that kept pushing him, provoking him…telling him both openly and subliminally that he would never learn what really happened the night Rick died.

And still, he'd wanted to kiss her?

Jon followed Sylvie out the door, the horror of his intentions smacking him like the dry, mountain air.

At home, he and Rick had never been competitive. He'd been preparing for college when his mother had announced her pregnancy. He'd just turned seventeen when Rick was born, his arrival a joy in the household. Jon had accepted his younger brother from the moment Rick first spat breast milk down the back of his favorite shirt.

This sudden need to kiss Sylvie wasn't born of jealousy. He refused to believe that. So what the hell was it born of, then?

Outside, the sun beat down on them. Squinting at Sylvie, he asked, "Do you have a hat? It's hot out here. You don't feel faint, do you?"

Sylvie stopped at the fence that enclosed the nearest paddock. She spun her heel in the dirt to face him. "Let's get one thing clear. First up, pregnant women can vomit at the drop of a hat and then feel like heaven for the rest of the day. I know. I've had eight weeks of doing just that. And secondly, I'll let my doctor and my own good sense tell me what I should and shouldn't do. All right?"

Good. She'd raised that defensive wall again. He needed that. "I don't want you to embarrass yourself in your own backyard, that's all."

She returned to her walking. When they reached the small barn closest to the house, she threw open the door and stepped into the dark building. He followed.

"I'll give you one thing, Jon. You're not intimidated by a tough woman, are you?"

He stepped into the dimness after her. "There won't be much you can do or say that will faze me, sweetheart, so don't bother scaring up all your worst military habits to try and oust me. My ex-wife was a social worker in Toronto's Chinatown. She was every bit as tough as you and I managed to hold my own with her."

"Before or after you two divorced?"

If he'd expected capitulation, he'd have been as big a fool as he'd been during his farce of a marriage. His ex-wife had been pregnant, into her second trimester and he hadn't even noticed. Had she hidden it that well, or had he just stopped caring?

Ahead, Sylvie had become a shadow in the dimly lit

barn. But he saw enough to notice her hand stray to her still-flat belly.

He crushed the urge to swear. Loudly. At Sylvie. She had exactly what he wanted. She could give him Rick's last hours, make that connection—be that connection—to his lost brother. She carried his only living relative and…she was also keeping a secret. He'd worked with enough suspects to know the difference between those who openly admitted they weren't going to talk, and those with a secret to keep.

But Sylvie fitted both and it pissed him off.

Inhaling the smells of hay and animals, he became thankful that she couldn't make out his features and guess his thoughts, in case she could read him as easily as he read her.

As his eyes adjusted to the dark, he searched for the words to gloss over the memory of that day his ex-wife announced she was carrying some other social worker's child. "My ability to hold my own with my wife had no bearing on our marriage or our divorce. We simply grew apart, living separate lives until she announced one day she was moving out. I couldn't think of a single good reason for her to stay."

She studied his face, exactly as he expected her to. "And you're telling me this because you want to show me you're sincere, right?"

For a moment he wasn't sure if she believed him or not. His words didn't even ring true in his own ears. "I'm not telling you this to prove anything. You asked," he finally answered.

She shrugged and turned her attention to a small room nearby.

Anger swelled in him. All of this foolishness could be

avoided, if Sylvie would tell him what he wanted to know. "How did Rick die?"

Sylvie stiffened as she swung away from him. "I told you I can't talk about it. I signed a nondisclosure agreement. You're familiar with those, aren't you? Legally binding documents that say you can't say anything—even if you want to? Look, I know you're hurting, but recounting Rick's last hours isn't going to bring him back. It's only going to torture you."

She didn't meet his steady gaze. She was hiding behind a rule, a contract, just like his ex-wife had hidden behind her own privacy when he'd asked her who the father was.

Sharply, he pulled the anger in. He wasn't angry with Tanya. She'd been lucky enough to find love again quickly. Her baby had been a shock and a complication, and he still wasn't sure how to take it, but now he focused on the fact that the kid would be loved and cared for.

Would Sylvie's baby have that good fortune? Of course. Whether she realized it or not, Sylvie was already displaying strong protective instincts. She wanted Rick's baby…and she didn't want him.

A knot formed in his stomach. "Your candor isn't going to shock me, Sylvie, so don't try to use it as a weapon."

Her expression suddenly softened. "Rick was like that, too. Never bothered by my forthrightness. I admired that in him. A lot of soldiers resented me and my attitude. I could never figure them out. They didn't mind women in the army, and would say we had to be 'one of the guys.' So I was one and they resented that. But Rick didn't care. He was—" she paused "—reasonable."

The knot tightened. "Reasonable? That's all you have? Rick was a hell of a lot more than reasonable. He had to have been to father that child of yours!'' He tried to clip his growing irritation, but hell, how could she just tag on some blasé term?

Sylvie reddened, a reaction he hadn't expected to see. He plowed on, regardless. ''Rick must have cared for you. He wasn't the kind of person who would screw a woman simply because it felt like a good idea.'' The coarse words tasted bitter on his tongue. He hated them. But looking at her go from red to white, he was glad he'd struck a nerve.

''I know what Rick was like. We did talk when we were stuck alone in that truck.''

''You did more than talk.''

''What we did and why we did it are none of your business.'' She narrowed her eyes. ''Who are you really mad at, here? Me, Rick, or the ex-wife you grew apart from?''

Any sharp retort he had inside snapped back at him like a taut rubber band. She spun away from him and bustled into a small room.

''We keep all the tools in here,'' she gritted out. ''I need you to fix the zoo paddock first. Bruce, he's the pot-bellied pig, keeps slipping under the fence. He's already dug through a camper's garbage. I'm thinking that if you take some of the wire that's behind the barn and bury it where he's been digging, we should thwart him good. When you've done that, the front steps need nailing down again.''

She was ready to leave him to his chores, stalk right past him, in fact, when she frowned at his clothes. ''You should change.''

He looked down at his shirt. He had packed one set of old shorts and a couple of T-shirts, in case he could squeeze in some jogging, but that was all. He hadn't figured he'd be sticking around all summer.

He looked into the toolroom. Well, at least he'd still be exercising.

"Sylvie?" A voice called from deep within the barn.

She slipped past Jon. "Yes, Lawrence?"

Jon followed her out of the toolroom. A tall, wiry, white-haired man appeared. He looked at Jon with a sharp frown.

Sylvie made the simplest of introductions. "Jon is the brother of one of the soldiers I knew in Bosnia."

Lawrence nodded, silently taking in Jon and his too-dressy-for-the-barn clothes. The old man turned back to Sylvie. "Heard you puking again this morning."

Jon also looked at him. Apparently, the idea of mincing words didn't exist on this ranch.

"You'll notice Lawrence has learned the Mitchell art of diplomacy," Sylvie said. "He's worked for my father and grandfather."

"I'm too old to beat around the bush."

Sylvie drew in a long breath, steeling her shoulders at the same time. "I'm surprised you've waited so long to say something. I'm pregnant, okay?"

Lawrence shrugged and headed into the small toolroom, talking as he went. "You want me to do the wagon tour tonight? The sign-up list at the office is full."

"Yes, thanks." She shut her eyes, and Jon watched her swallow.

Behind both of them, Lawrence chuckled. "Hard to believe after all those rough roads and ol' army trucks, you're brought to your knees by a homemade prairie schooner and a simple pregnancy."

"Thanks, Lawrence, you always make me feel better."

He turned to Jon. "Here camping?"

"Sylvie offered me a job for the summer."

"Really?" Lawrence squinted at him. "Can you ride?"

Jon glanced over at Sylvie, who also waited for his reply. "I did a two-year stint with the mounted unit in Toronto."

Lawrence quirked an eyebrow at Sylvie, who added, "Jon's a police officer in Toronto. But he's only needed here to do the yard work and general maintenance. I don't see any reason to have him riding around with you all day."

"Then you may want him to run into town with you. The shipping company called. Your unaccompanied baggage has finally arrived."

"Good. It's about time." She smiled at Lawrence. Hardly broad, it was gentle, patient, so different. "Why don't you help me with it? I have a gift for you in it."

Lawrence chuckled and smiled back.

Now that was interesting. She was obviously very attached to the old man. Jon tucked that mental note away for future possibilities.

But the old man shook his head. "Not today, I'm afraid. We've got four stupid head of cattle that have broken through the fence and wandered up the trail. They gave three hikers quite a scare when they chased them."

Jon spoke up. "I'll take you into town, Sylvie. It'll give me a chance to buy more appropriate clothes. And you can get your car, *if* you're feeling up to driving home, that is."

At his subtle challenge, she shot him a suspicious look. Then, catching sight of the uplifted corner of his mouth, the look shifted. Her smooth, lush lips parted, her eyes widened.

The mote-filled air around them heated and thickened. And the moment lingered.

Jon stared at her. In his line of work, he only ever saw the innocent, haunted look Sylvie now wore on the faces of child victims.

Innocent? Surely he was mistaken. He had to be missing something here. Damn it, something to do with Rick?

He stared harder at her, silently willing her to speak. *Tell me what you can't say, Sylvie.*

She blinked away the haunted expression, and immediately the coolness returned. "Sure we can go now. I'm fine."

No, she wasn't, his intuition whispered. Jon pursed his lips into a tight line. Maybe the look had been a product of heat and hormones. Pregnant women glowed, they said.

"Then it's settled," Lawrence said, oblivious to the disturbing undercurrent flowing between Jon and Sylvie. "Better take the truck."

Jon mentally yanked himself from his thoughts. He gave Sylvie his best poker face. "Yeah. Ready?"

Sylvie cleared her throat and nodded. She walked past the two men, Jon pivoting to watch her leave.

Was she really a victim here? She had been in the truck with Rick when it had been ambushed. Victim *was* the correct word.

So why was he here, waiting for just the right moment to squeeze out the private secrets of Rick's last hours, in total violation of the legally binding agreement she'd signed?

What the hell kind of person was he?

A man in need of the truth, that's what. The truth from a woman keeping more than a secret hidden inside of her.

"Oh, hey, Jon," Lawrence interrupted his desperate thoughts. The old man scratched a stubby growth of beard. "Um, the library is right beside the shipping company. I'm going to call in and have a few books signed out. Would you mind picking them up while Sylvie's getting her stuff? Under the name of Lawrence Fawcett. The librarian will know."

Sylvie shoved open the barn door and escaped outside, inhaling the mountain breeze with hope it would clear her mind. She hadn't wanted to go into town with Jon, suspecting he'd find it the perfect time to pump her for details she'd rather not give. *Rather not?* More likely, *never* give.

But when he lifted one corner of his mouth, with challenge in his eyes, she'd felt a stirring within.

God, he was gorgeous. It hadn't really struck her until that moment. Suddenly, one night of passion—one of the most inappropriate events ever—had transformed her from...

She swallowed. From cool virgin to full, sensual woman.

Her temples pounded. She hadn't wanted to get involved with Rick.

Until she faced death as a virgin.

Oh, Lord. She'd been so incredibly selfish. A man was dead just because she hadn't wanted to die a virgin, and now she was pregnant, alone, and of all things, fatally attracted to her one-time lover's bitter brother, who was hinting that he wanted to be a father to the child.

Wasn't that dandy?

Directly in her vision stood the back of the house, or more pointedly, the kitchen. Had Jon actually considered kissing her? *No.* It was grief, and the way the shadows played on his face. For all she knew, he'd mastered the hungry sexual look years ago, and now wore it as a matter of habit.

"Are the keys in the truck?"

She jumped, knocking her attention from the house to Jon, who'd slipped up beside her, completely unnoticed.

"Sorry. I didn't mean to scare you."

She tried to look calm. "It's all right."

The truck sat silent in front of her, its dark-green paint faded in spots by the brutal Alberta sun. Beside Jon, in a truck, while he drove?

His dark profile would show his concentration on his driving, like Rick's had.

A sharp squeal cut through the hot air. She spun around to find the source.

Immediately Jon caught her arm. His warm fingers wrapped around her elbow as he pointed to the part of the front yard they could see. "It's just the pig entertaining the kids. Relax."

She sagged, letting out a whoosh of air. Of course. It was just Bruce. It wasn't that night—

She offered Jon a foolish, wobbly smile. "Bruce is the camp favorite. But I swear if he roots through one more bag of garbage, there'll be a pig roast on the next long weekend."

Jon's eyebrows creased together ever so briefly before he smiled and released her elbow. "Shall I drive?"

"No," she snapped. Abruptly she cleared her throat and stiffened the smile she'd forced on her face. "Thanks. I'll drive. I know where to go."

When they reached the shipping company, Jon threw open the cab door. The bright sun beat down on him as he turned to face her. "I'll just go get those books Lawrence asked for, then I'll be straight back. Don't lift anything, even if they say you have to, okay? I'll do it.''

He threw her the firmest look he could summon after the relaxing ride back into town. She merely shrugged. ''Suit yourself.''

Jon climbed out and slammed the door. Sylvie had been quiet on the trip in. Her insistence on driving hadn't struck him as odd, until they sat inside the old rattletrap and he'd realized that it was possible the last time she'd been riding as a passenger in a big truck was with Rick. And Rick, being the subordinate, would have done the driving.

She hadn't wanted Jon to drive, and he understood her choice.

Walking across the pavement and through the scattering of various cars, he wiped his forehead with the back of his hand. Thankfully, he had the experience of Toronto in the dog days of August. Now that was hot, especially in a bulletproof vest and dark pants. Here was a dry heat, he told himself. Tolerable.

So why didn't he feel cooler? It was just barely June, for crying out loud.

A chorus of laughter and noise greeted him as he entered the library. An elderly librarian was reading a story to a circle of youngsters, all of whom yelled out excitedly when a question arose in the book's dialogue. Preschool morning, he presumed. He walked up to the counter. ''I'm here to pick up some books for a Lawrence Fawcett.''

The librarian nodded and pulled three books from under the counter. ''They've already been signed out, so you don't need anything. Here's the slip saying when they have to be back.'' She showed him the narrow paper before tucking it into the top book. ''Tell Lawrence I've bought a whole bunch of new westerns he might be interested in. Especially after reading these books.''

Jon glanced down at the short pile, his eyes widening. *Breastfeeding—Nature's Way.* He lifted the book and read the next title. *A Father's Guide to Surviving Pregnancy.* Almost too scared to look, he lifted the second book and peered down. *Pregnancy and Birth—An In-Depth Look at the Details.* Wonderful. Why couldn't Lawrence have asked Sylvie to fetch them?

He scooped up the books. Jeez, she'd just told him this morning. Was Lawrence already planning to be Sylvie's labor coach? Dazed, he walked back to the shipping company, stopping only to dump the books on the front seat of the truck. Over the hood he spied Sylvie, lifting a large duffel bag over her shoulder. At her feet were two large barrack boxes and a rucksack.

What the hell was she doing?

He swore, long and loud enough for her to hear him. ''Damn it, woman, I said I'd do that!''

He jogged over to the cement docking ramp and leaped up to glare at the young, pimply faced worker beside her. ''What's wrong with you, anyway? She's pregnant, you know. And you're making her lift all of this by herself?''

The worker blinked. ''No, sir. I was going to put it all on a pallet and forklift onto her truck. I didn't know she was pregnant. Sorry.''

Jon drew in a tight seethe. Of course he wouldn't know. And he bet Sylvie wouldn't ask for help.

Sylvie threw the lightly stuffed bag onto the wooden pallet the worker had hastily retrieved. ''Good grief, Jon, quit ragging on the kid. I know my limitations, all right? This duffel bag's practically empty.''

''The rest of it will be heavy. I know. I've got all of Rick's stuff still sitting on my living room floor.''

She grabbed the shipping order and scrawled out her signature, tearing off her copy with the ease of someone who had worked in shipping all her adult life. Folding it with clipped, jerky movements, she snapped, "You still have his stuff in your living room? I packed his boxes two days after he died. They left by Hercules aircraft the day we had his memorial service. Isn't it about time you sorted through that stuff? You're only delaying the inevitable."

Without waiting for his answer, she stalked down the steps to the truck.

Her expression still grim, she backed up the pickup, lining it up beside to the dock. Behind Jon, the young worker, now in the forklift, threw him a cautious look before carrying the pallet down a long ramp. When he reached the truck, he loaded the baggage onto the truck's bed. "Um, I need the pallet back sometime, Ms. Mitchell." He turned to Jon. "Is this all right?"

"Fine," he muttered. Her stuff looked exactly like Rick's. Rick's stuff had had bright blue strips of cloth tied to the handles of the barrack boxes and duffel bag. Probably in order to easily recognize them in the sea of olive green Jon could imagine lined the floor of a Hercules cargo plane.

Sylvie's strips of material were the same color.

Sweat beaded on his forehead. Yet his insides chilled him. He hadn't received Rick's stuff until six weeks after he'd buried him. And then, sick of not getting the answers he needed, and encouraged by his chief, he'd dumped his brother's effects into his living room and called the airline. All that was left of Rick's life had been sitting in his living room for almost a month.

Damn it, Rick deserved better.

Jon searched the horizon, a flat line broken up by the

outline of the library beyond. Could Sylvie be right? Had he been delaying the inevitable? But to go through all of Rick's things, every last scrap? What the hell would he do with it all? Longing ached his bones. Damn it, Rick, why did you have to die so young?

He studied Sylvie's profile in the back window of the truck as she peered into the bed at something. How had she felt, sorting through her lover's clothes and uniforms, packing up his personal items?

Being one hell of a woman, Sylvie would have managed, just as she'd manage parenthood. But she couldn't give her baby the one thing he deserved: someone who could tell him about his father.

Already he was thinking of the kid as a male. A boy, a lively blond boy just like Rick. A boy who needed a man in his life, like Jon and Rick had needed their own father even before some coward killed him.

Jon had no idea how he would manage it, but damn it, he'd be that father figure for Rick's baby.

And as far as he was concerned, Sylvie didn't have a choice in the matter.

Chapter 4

Her grip tight on the steering wheel, Sylvie swallowed the wad of torment inside of her, wondering if it would ever shrink to a more manageable size. When had she turned so mean?

When Jon climbed into the truck beside her, his expression sober, she squirmed in her seat. With careful precision, she shifted the transmission into drive and eased away from the docking ramp. "Jon, I'm sorry for what I said."

There, it was out. And yes, it hurt.

He said nothing and she turned to him. "Did you hear me?"

"Yes." He kept staring straight ahead.

That was it? Jon Cahill didn't strike her as the sulky type, so what was he doing?

She shook her head in exasperation. "I was out of line saying that stuff about Rick's personal effects. You should take all the time you need to go through them."

He turned to her, his eyes dull and cheerless. "You packed them. You know there wasn't much there." He tightened his jaw and blinked. "It could wait."

"Yes, he hadn't taken a lot with him. He didn't figure he needed it. And some of his kit had to be returned to our company stores." She cleared her throat. "But there were some things that were important to him and I didn't want anyone else going through it."

"Did Rick keep a journal?"

The question squeezed the lump back into her throat. "I...I don't know. I didn't find one. Did he mention one?"

Jon studied her face. She tried to hold her expression still. If Rick had kept a journal, the last day of his life wouldn't have been recorded. *Thank God.*

"No," Jon said, still watching her. "I was only hoping I might find one. To help me understand your relationship better." It was his turn to clear his throat. "You might have become my sister-in-law."

Whoa. Big-time whoa. She wasn't going to be anyone's sister-in-law. No way. And with a maturity that belied his youth, Rick knew, too, what kind of relationship he had with her. They'd always been supervisor and subordinate. Friendly, professional...until that night.

It had been an emotionally difficult night for both of them, and she knew she had to protect Rick's privacy. He'd pushed for something Sylvie had actually wanted to give. A gift given only under the most terrible of circumstances.

She shuddered. Her body had accepted Rick's own gift, as if by some strange force it knew how much time he had left on earth.

Fury surged through her. They should have spent their

time trying to save both their lives, instead of creating a new one.

Damn the military for sending them up that mountain.

Thankful the medical center appeared, Sylvie loosened her death grip on the steering wheel and turned into the parking lot. She had to take hold of her anger and her reaction to the injustice of that night.

"Here. Do you think you can get home by yourself?" she asked, her tone brisk. "I have an errand to run, and I'd like to use my car."

He narrowed his eyes slightly, not in a suspicious way, but rather as if he were attempting to discern what was churning inside of her. "Sure, no problem. Where do you want me to put your stuff?"

"In the spare bedroom. Lawrence will show you." She tried to smile, but when she felt as though nothing could be squeezed from her, she gave up. "Thanks for all your help. I appreciate it." Grabbing the small knapsack that doubled as a purse, she hopped out.

Jon waited while she started her car. She offered him a casual wave and pretended to dig through her knapsack for something, all the while keeping one eye on the truck. It moved off.

Once Jon had disappeared around the bend of the road, Sylvie shut off the car engine. Now was the time to complete that errand.

She hurried into the birthing center, hoping she wasn't too late for the admin staff. A different young woman sat at the front desk, helping a couple ahead of her. Sylvie waited until it was her turn.

The woman offered her a smile. "Can I help you?"

She tried to speak, but the words stuck in her throat. She was only here to find out about prenatal classes. It was something that could have waited until she saw the doctor on Wednesday, but when she'd seen the medical center again, she'd wanted to do it now. So how could it be so difficult?

"Is there something I can help you with?"

Oh, this was foolish. She straightened her shoulders. "I'm here to find out when the next prenatal classes are."

The woman pulled a booklet from her drawer and flipped through it. "There's one starting two weeks from Tuesday, and they run every other week after that. Can I put your name down?"

"Yes. Sylvie Mitchell."

"And your husband's name?"

She blinked and pursed her lips. "There is no husband."

"Oh." The woman looked as if such a thing wasn't possible. "But the father can…should come…." The receptionist trailed off, smiling blandly.

Sylvie's voice came out tight. "He won't be coming to any classes." Jeez, it sounded so stupid to say that. "I'll be having this baby alone."

The woman looked confused. And uncomfortable. "Oh. But you shouldn't. The course information states you need a labor partner. A coach."

"That would be me."

Sylvie spun around, knowing as she turned who stood behind her.

Jon—filling all too well the entrance to the small reception area.

Couldn't he leave her alone? Wasn't it enough that he'd finagled a summer job out of her? Did he have to constantly be there, reminding her of the mistakes she'd made?

As if she needed reminding. All those sleepless nights,

plus she hadn't had a decent breakfast all week, not to mention the ache starting in her hip ligaments.

"What are you doing here?"

His expression chilled her. "You forget who I am. I make it my business to know when people are lying."

"That doesn't explain why you're here."

"I drove around the block. The way you said you needed to do an errand made me…" He trailed off and, working his jaw, he finished, "Let's just say I was interested in what errand you had to do without me."

"Oh, come on, I was hardly lying to you. It's none of your business what errands I have to run."

"Perhaps not, but to you, you were lying. And I wanted to know why." He lifted his eyebrows. "Some people can lie like a sidewalk. You're not one of them."

"I'll have to work on that," she said dryly, turning around again to speak to the interested receptionist. "Like I said, I have no labor partner. If I get one, I'll let you know."

"What's wrong with me?"

She turned to face him again. "You won't be around. I'm not due until December."

"But I'll be around for your prenatal classes. And you need a breathing coach."

"No, I don't." Again she turned, annoyed at the dizziness all her spinning had caused.

"So, if I'm not going to be around for the delivery, what's the problem? I'll help out in the meantime."

His tone was so bland, she nearly believed his words. Nearly. Thirteen years in the military had taught her not to trust Jon's casual words.

Still, Jon was nothing if not tenacious. He was determined to prove his sincerity, and the displays so far had gone a long way to that end, she had to admit.

And how had she repaid him for it? With cruel words. And refusing to help him find the closure he desperately wanted.

Why couldn't he just accept Rick's death and move on? She knew all too well that he wasn't going to find peace in the truth she had to keep to herself.

But he was right about one thing. He wasn't going to be around for the delivery, so what difference would it make if he accompanied her to some prenatal classes? He would see a few extended bellies, listen to some dry facts on motherhood, and he'd soon be gone. If he lasted that long.

"Fine. Suit yourself." She met the curious receptionist's gaze and flicked up her hand. "Make that two of us. Sylvie Mitchell and Jon Cahill." She spelled out his last name.

She took the narrow pamphlet on the course and shoved it into Jon's hard chest. "This is for you. Keep every other Tuesday evening open."

Out in the sunshine, Jon watched Sylvie start up her car and drive away. Had she been considering someone else for the role of coach? Her father? No, more likely Lawrence.

Or a boyfriend? A man who'd already told her he'd help her raise her child? Be a father to it?

He gritted his teeth. Too bad. This child was *his* nephew or niece, *his* only link to his brother. He might not raise the baby, but he was at least going to strengthen his connection to the little thing, and the best way to start that was to attend prenatal classes.

Still, the idea of a boyfriend waiting somewhere sat like a stone inside of him. Another man involved in his brother's child's life? Giving advice, hugs…

Backrubs to the mother?

Hey, Jon, that's not your concern. The inner voice rang so clearly, he wondered if the young family passing him on his way to the truck might have heard it.

He should get used to the fact Sylvie didn't want him around, because come September, he wouldn't be.

At the truck, he toed the dirt that had been blown by the constant wind into a small dune beside his tire. The only reason Sylvie accepted him was because of his bulldozer attitude. And the fact she needed a laborer.

But if his bulldozing attitude continued, he could see Sylvie putting her foot down pretty damn quick. Oh, yeah, right down on him, like a bug.

Feeling the sun beat hot on his head, Jon decided it was best if he bought his work clothes and got back to the ranch. No doubt Sylvie would notice his absence, and not in a fond way.

Less than an hour later he found Lawrence inside the small front corral, coaxing a suspicious pot-bellied pig to come close to the fence. Several barefoot children, obviously campers, stretched tiny arms through the rails, each begging the animal to take their treats. The pig must have had his fill of garbage because he wasn't budging.

"Hey, Lawrence," he called out after he'd parked the truck and approached the corral. "If you're not busy, can you show me where to put Sylvie's UAB?"

Lawrence lifted his head and frowned. "UAB?"

"Sylvie's unaccompanied baggage from Bosnia."

"Oh, yeah." Lawrence said something to the kids before leaving the corral. "Sure. Did you get my books?"

"Yes. Are you actually going to read that stuff?"

"Why not? Somebody's gotta know what's going on around here. And if you think Sylvie'll read them, I've got some land to sell you."

Jon shook his head at the vision he couldn't quite form in his head. A crusty old farmhand reading maternity books.

But then again, as a police officer, he'd seen pretty much the weirdest stuff. Lawrence wasn't harming anyone and maybe he was on the right track.

"Sylvie said to put her stuff in the spare bedroom."

"Hmm." The old man scratched the growth of stubble on his chin. "I guess we'll be calling the spare bedroom the nursery before long." After he grabbed a duffel bag off the truck, he threw open the front door and stalked inside. It took Jon a few minutes to adjust to the dim interior, but carrying a barrack box, he managed to follow the old man down the hallway to the end room.

"Best room for a nursery, I guess. Gets the morning sun. The afternoon sun gets too hot 'round here. And this room connects with Sylvie's, anyway." Lawrence let out a dry chuckle. "That way she won't disturb her pa."

And his new wife? Jon couldn't help but mentally add that phrase for Lawrence. He followed the old hand's gaze to the open connecting door. Beyond stood a neat, well-made bed, plain and orderly. No fancy pillows or childhood toys for Sylvie. A nightstand beside the bed held a clock, a chain and dog tags. And a stack of disposable tissues.

Curious. Jon scanned the room for a wastebasket. He found it over in the far corner, holding a scrunched-up tissue carton, its whimsical design clearly visible.

A teddy bear in army fatigues, driving an army truck. Sylvie had taken the time to remove, refold and stack all of the tissues. And then she'd crushed the box into the size of a deck of cards.

Curious indeed.

"Seen enough? Or are you waiting for me to bring in all the UAB?"

Jon jerked back and cleared his throat. "No."

Lawrence squinted at him. "You married, son?"

"Divorced."

"Then a woman's room shouldn't be a mystery to you. Let's go."

As Lawrence walked ahead of Jon, he continued, "Now, me, I'm a whole different breed. Never been married. Don't know a damn thing about women."

"That'll change as soon as you start into one of those books." He'll learn way more than he ever wanted to.

Lawrence nodded. "Yep. Expect that to be true. Not that I don't understand Sylvie. She's a Mitchell through and through. Stubborn, tough lot. Her pa used to be like that, too, till he got himself married a second time. Andrea softened him up, but good. I guess the right spouse can do just about anything."

"You've known Sylvie long?"

"All her life."

He followed the man outside. "Why did she join the military? I mean, her father has this ranch. I would think she'd want to stay on it."

Lawrence stopped at the edge of the porch steps. "The ranch wasn't doing so good back then. They were tough times back thirteen years. A lot of ranches were lost with high interest rates and all. Allister struggled, too. Sylvie wanted him to sell. She was just a kid, full of ideas and knowing everything. Teenagers aren't all that big on heritage, either."

"But she's back here now."

Lawrence paused by the truck, nodding pensively. "Yeah, she is."

For a moment he looked miles away, his eyes narrowing slightly, his leathery face wrinkled into a frown. Jon was about to prompt him, knowing by instinct that something important lingered just below the surface.

But Lawrence cleared his throat as he pulled another square, olive-drab barrack box from the truck bed. "Yeah, she came home, all right. And the minute she got out of her car, I knew she wasn't the same kid that left for Bosnia."

"She wasn't a kid, either."

Lawrence smiled at him, looking like a hound dog whose jowls had been held back by some mischievous child. "Anyone under fifty is a kid, son."

"Was Bosnia Sylvie's only overseas tour?"

Lawrence snapped out of his reverie. "Heck, no. She's been to the Golan Heights in the Middle East. And three months in Afghanistan, too. I figured she'd come back changed after that one, but she didn't. Still the same opinionated Sylvie. Now, this time, I don't know. She's quieter, more mature." He grinned abruptly. "Heck, it may be just the baby doing it to her. I'll let you know after I've read those books."

Good luck, Jon thought. Not the sort of reading material he cared for. He had the latest *Sports Illustrated* in his suitcase, right beside one of Tom Clancy's newest. That was his limit on gruesome.

"I'll get the suitcase. You take the heavier stuff. You're younger than me." Lawrence swung the barrack box around and shoved it into Jon's midriff.

The air left his lungs in one giant whoosh. Lawrence may be in his eighties, and built like a line of barbwire, but he was as strong as any man Jon knew.

The old man chuckled. "Don't let Sylvie see you wimping out like that. She isn't the sort to tolerate such nonsense."

"What nonsense?"

Both men turned to face the voice. Sylvie strode toward them, a confident, defiant stride that bore a touch of wariness he figured only he could detect. Lawrence might see a milder, matured version of Sylvie, but he saw a strong, suspicious woman. One determined to keep him, even though he was the uncle of her child, as distant as possible.

She carried his only relative. He took the moment to imagine her heavy with child, full, lush breasts and softer, rounded features. Glowing and healthy, teeming with womanhood.

His ex-wife had almost looked as good the day they'd signed their divorce papers. Holy-moly. The last time he was involved with a woman, she, too, was carrying another man's child.

And the way his breath caught and his jeans ached, he knew he couldn't lie to himself. He was getting involved with Sylvie.

He snapped his attention away from her and scanned the circular driveway for her car, spying it at the far end, away from the small throng of camping children who'd chosen the dust of the road over the sandbox.

"So what nonsense are you two talking about?" she asked again.

"Nothing," he answered before Lawrence could speak.

"Your new hand can't handle a bit of decent work, Sylvie," Lawrence said, anyway. "Why'd ya hire him? He's a wimpy city boy."

Jon threw the man a sharp glare, one the smiling Lawrence pointedly ignored as he added, "If there's not more to do here, I've got tack to clean." He hauled the last of the UAB onto his shoulder and sauntered into the house.

Jon turned to Sylvie. Her eyebrows lifted in watchful curiosity, and he wondered if it would be worth the bother to defend himself. But before he could mind his tongue, he said, "He's exaggerating. I can handle anything you throw at me."

She made no comment. But, very briefly, her gaze flicked down his frame and up again.

Wrong thing to say. To any other woman he knew, such a small, sexual innuendo would have yielded a smile. To Sylvie, his words seemed to skitter around her like water on hot pavement.

And yet her eyelids lowered as her jaw relaxed and the barest flush pinkened her cheeks. Was she actually assessing the temptation?

Damn, he'd have to be more careful. He wasn't usually so loose-lipped, even with the female officers he'd worked with, those who could give as good as they got, sometimes throwing in a tempting offer of their own. Such banter wasn't his style, and he didn't want a repeat of that brief episode in the kitchen where he'd actually considered kissing her.

Thankfully, the heat in her eyes cooled, replaced by tired caution. She showed no suggestion that she'd even caught the innuendo.

"I'm sure you can do all the work you've been hired to do. Of course, if you can't, you'll be fired." After that bland, tired-sounding warning, she walked past him into the house.

Sylvie needed to lie down. *Now.* Her feet and her head ached, and the queasiness in between had returned with a vengeance. A dark room and a cold compress sounded so heavenly she nearly cried for it.

A *really* cold compress, she decided, considering what

Jon had said. Oh, yes, she didn't doubt he could handle anything she threw at him. Anything at all.

Good grief, she needed to rest. She must be absolutely exhausted if the idea of a good, hard man had cut to the top of her list of needs.

As soon as she entered her room, she pulled the drapes shut and flaked out on the bed with a groan.

Sleep, she ordered her body. *Forget everything and sleep so long that when you wake up, all your problems will have been sorted out.*

A sharp noise from beyond her door hit her pounding temples. Instantly she leaped up and grappled at the air beside her bed.

"What the Sam Hill—"

Chapter 5

Sylvie cut off her own words when she spied Jon standing in the center of the adjoining room.

She shut her mouth to the foul curse that could have easily burst from her lips. Then, forcing her eyes to close tightly, she attempted to will her heart rate back to normal. Such scares could hardly be good for the baby.

"What," she breathed out on one long exhale, "did you just do? Set off a cannon?" She was almost too scared to open her eyes, afraid she'd find her belongings, her world, in tiny fragments around Jon.

Maybe it wouldn't be such a bad idea to start afresh.

"I'm sorry." His smooth deep voice sliced through her body as easily as a warm knife through butter. "I didn't mean to scare you."

She dared to open her eyes. He stood near the adjoining door, watching her all too attentively with that damn cool, inquisitive expression.

Good grief, he was nothing like his brother. Rick

would never stare at her with a look so close to—what the heck was it—suspicion? Rick would have smiled, apologized smoothly and returned to his work.

"The box slipped from my hands just as I was setting it down. I only dropped it a few inches. Would there be anything breakable in it?"

She sighed. "No." All of her furniture and effects had been shipped back to the ranch before she began her tour of duty. She knew she'd be retiring immediately after. Jon would eat off her favorite china at suppertime when he showed up for the meal the housekeeper had prepared last night, if Sylvie had enough energy to heat the stuff up. "It's all right."

It wasn't all right, but what else could she say? He hadn't dropped the box deliberately. Fatigue had made her testy.

"I guess you're tired, eh?"

She lifted her eyebrows and let another sigh waffle through her. "Yes. Look," she said, gesturing carelessly to the numerous boxes and kit bags scattered about her future nursery. "Just dump what's left in the hallway. We'll worry about them all later." She stifled a yawn as she turned back to the welcoming bed.

"That's it."

She looked over her shoulder at him. "Hmm?"

"There are no more boxes."

For a moment she stood in the middle of her room, not more than four feet from him, and wondered what the heck he was talking about.

"This is all your unaccompanied baggage," he elaborated.

"Oh." Good grief, she must be beat. Feeling a bit stupid, she offered Jon a simple smile and returned to the bed.

He followed her, only to stop at the threshold. And lying on her bed, with her eyes shut, she could still sense him watching her.

To hell with it. She wasn't the shy, modest type. That type never lasted in the army, where you might find yourself sharing a tent with just about any other noncommissioned officer. She'd spent the first three months in Bosnia sharing an ISO, a large metal box resembling a sea container, with a female cook. The last three months, through a miserable cold winter, after several ISOs had been shipped to another camp, she lived with two drivers and Rick—

She tightened her jaw. Had he lived, would they have resumed their platonic relationship, knowing that they'd—that she was carrying his child?

But he hadn't lived.

Her stomach heaved and she threw open her eyes. "Is there anything else you need?" she asked, pushing away the horror on the off chance Jon might really be able to read her mind.

With his shoulder pressed against the door frame, he folded his arms. He looked as though he belonged here, for Pete's sake. As if he didn't need an invitation to enter her bedroom.

She slammed shut the lid on that thought.

Finally he spoke. "Nothing. I was going to ask you if you needed anything to make yourself more comfortable."

There he went, insinuating himself into her life. She'd only known him a few hours and he seemed fully prepared to take over the role of father to her child.

Forget it. And forget about thinking of all the other duties he might perform. He'll be gone in September.

Rolling over, she stared at the far wall, where several

busy landscapes Andrea had painted hung. "No, I'm fine. I just need to rest for a few minutes."

But however she felt didn't stop him from watching her with that dark, suspicious-cop expression, the one that rolled around her like a cold draft. She twisted back. "Stop that!"

He lifted his brows. "Stop what?"

"Stop looking at me like a cop."

"I didn't realize that I was." He offered a careless smile. Briefly, a glimpse of Rick danced over his expression. She shut her eyes, wishing there wasn't such an indefinable resemblance.

No, Jon was uniquely himself.

Riding in on a moment of warm fatigue, a fantasy of him kneading away her tension drifted over her.

"I just want to be alone for a few minutes, okay?" She forced out her words, praying they'd dispel that damn tempting vision.

Silence answered her, until the sound of Jon clicking shut the door sliced through her brain. Without peeking through half-closed eyelids, she knew he'd left her alone.

Alone with her regret and a headache.

And a fantasy that had inexplicably soothed her in a way she figured she'd never be soothed.

By the time the sun had moved over to glare into his face, Jon was ready to quit for the day. He worked out regularly in Toronto, but here, outside with the strong wind and sun, hauling fencing, pounding poles and completing the chores Sylvie had assigned him, he needed a break.

He tore off his new Stetson and wiped his brow, recalling how he'd quietly shut Sylvie's bedroom door and headed outside, all the while mentally organizing his agenda. Do the work, get settled in the bunkhouse, then call his shift sergeant to confirm his leave arrangements. Then, if he was still standing, he'd call the neighbor who was minding his house while he was gone.

Static on the two-way radio Lawrence had offered told him the old man was trying to reach him. Jon moved into the open field and keyed the send button.

"Lawrence? You trying to call me?"

The old man's voice cut through the static. "Yup. Supper's ready. Main house. You can clean up in the back porch."

Finally. But the main house? Did that mean Sylvie was responsible for feeding them?

He thinned his lips. She hadn't been in any shape to even stand up, let alone cook a meal for a bunch of hungry men. He climbed onto the ATV and headed back across the dry landscape toward the house.

Fifteen minutes later he found Sylvie hovering over the stove, swiping her brow as she stirred the contents of a deep pot. Its scent filled the air, a savory mix of Italian seasonings, tomatoes and rich meat, rivaling any of the delicious dishes he could sample in Toronto. "Smells great," he announced as he stepped into the kitchen.

She eyed his hat before speaking. "Marg can whip up the greatest Italian dishes." She moved a large bowl of steaming pasta to the center of the table, beside a wide tray of bubbling cheese bread.

"Marg?"

"Our housekeeper. She comes in Mondays and Thursdays, cleans the entire house and prepares enough food to feed all of us until she comes back. All I have to do is throw it in the oven, or reheat it." She glanced at him, her eyebrows raised. "You didn't think I slaved over a hot stove all afternoon?"

Yes, he had, and he hadn't liked it. And how did he feel now that he learned she wasn't responsible for the tempting food in front of them? Relieved?

Yeah, of course he was relieved. Now he wouldn't have to play the bad guy and order her to rest.

He cleared his throat. When had he ever balked at being tough?

When he'd seen that butting heads with Sylvie would only widen the rift in their already-uneasy relationship.

Hell, relationships, especially those with women, weren't exactly his forte. He'd blown it with his ex-wife, leaving him to take his women like he took his coffee breaks—few and far between.

He glanced at Lawrence who watched his lengthening silence with interest. He looked again at Sylvie. "I'm glad you didn't have to cook, but I saw you here and figured you'd felt better after I left, that's all."

She wiped her hands on the boldly printed apron tied around her waist. It didn't match her style, so he figured it must be Marg's. "I rested a bit, but I'm not used to lounging around all day. So I got up, threw this stuff in the oven and started unpacking."

She smiled across at Lawrence, who'd already sat down and begun helping himself to the pitcher of dark-red juice in front of him. "I found your present, Lawrence. Want it now?"

"Nope. After supper would be better. Jon and I worked like the dickens this afternoon, and I'm looking to feed myself first and foremost." He pulled out a chair. "Sit down, Jon, you make a man nervous."

Jon shot a glance at Sylvie, as she sat herself down across from Lawrence. There were three other chairs, and, judging by the sounds from the back porch, the other two ranch hands were cleaning up. Jon chose the chair beside Sylvie.

She smelled like tomatoes and bread, and he wondered if she hadn't done more than she'd claimed.

"Let's hope you feel better soon, Sylvie," Lawrence said as the other men sat down. "We'll need you out at the line shack. We have to make a decision on it in the next couple of weeks. I'd like to see it torn down, but we still need the damn thing."

Jon grabbed some cheese bread from the tray that one of the other men, Purley, handed him. "Where's this line shack?"

"A few miles west of here." Lawrence helped himself to pasta and sauce. "Right close to where the trails begin. Tough terrain, though. Up and down."

Sylvie must have seen his confused expression. "Our land ends at the line shack. It's government land after that and we keep the rights to graze the cattle there, but more important, we have access to those national walking trails through K-country, that's the park area half a mile west of the line shack. Purley takes any campers who can ride up there. They get the choice of either riding the trails or herding cattle." She accepted the tray of bread from Jon, keeping her hands well away from his, he noted. "Did you get a carpenter to look at that shack, Lawrence?"

"Don't need a carpenter to tell me that mess of lumber is ready to be bulldozed."

"We need something out there. It's a long ways in on a bad day, especially if you've been riding the trails all day. And it's right beside the well." She stopped. "But we can't do anything until the end of the camping season. How about I ride out and check it in the next week or so? It'll give me an idea of what I'm talking about when I call the carpenter.''

"Suit yourself." Lawrence dug into his meal.

Jon couldn't believe what he'd heard. "You're going to ride out? As on a horse? Are you nuts? You can't ride all the way out there. Lawrence said the terrain's rough.''

Sylvie threw him a lethal look. A heavy silence dropped like a boulder on the huge kitchen. The two men, Purley and Michael, froze, their forks halfway between their plates and their open mouths. Lawrence lifted his eyebrows, obviously amused, it appeared.

Jon ignored them all. "When was the last time you rode a horse?''

Color flooded into Sylvie's cheeks. "I'm fine. This isn't any of your concern.''

"It is." He didn't elaborate, but from the intensifying glare, he knew she understood his meaning.

She glanced at Lawrence, but he cleared his throat. "I'm with Jon on this one, Sylvie. You haven't rode since last fall when you came home on that embarkation leave you got before Bosnia.''

Sylvie's mouth formed a thin line, and Jon felt a pang of sympathy for her. A damn large pang, too, but not large enough to back down. She'd returned home after a career in the army, no doubt hoping to run this ranch, and now was being coddled like a baby. One taste of her tough disposition and he knew she hadn't been pampered in the military and didn't want to be now.

But she was pregnant, damn it. Hadn't she considered that?

"You know," Lawrence continued, "I'm no expert here, but if you'd been riding regularly since fall, I'd say sure, continue. But you haven't. I don't think any woman in your condition should start something new.''

"It's not new. I've ridden all my life."

Lawrence set down his fork. "Hon, you haven't," he told her quietly. "You rode for the first seventeen years of your life. For the last thirteen, you've only ridden whenever you came home for a visit. And we both know those visits were few and far between."

Sylvie cast a furtive look down the table, where the two other hands were already digging into the excellent meal, their focuses on their food. Jon felt her sharp look glance off him on the return trip back to Lawrence. Her lips tightened and again the sympathy struck him.

She set her fork down. "Lawrence, you'd listen to a man you didn't know existed yesterday?"

"Nope, but I'd listen to a man who has some common sense."

"Fine, since your man will be using the pickup, I'll take the ATV." She threw a challenging look at Jon. "And don't tell me an ATV is no good for me, either. I've been riding around in four-wheel-drive ten-ton trucks for the past thirteen years. Done nothing but that for the last six months." Her voice hitched abruptly. "I think I can handle an ATV."

Jon started to smile, to offer her something encouraging, but catching her glare, he carefully hid his satisfaction behind a huge bite of bread.

"Be careful of the ATV," Lawrence warned, unruffled by her fume. "It's been acting up lately."

Quiet reigned through the rest of the meal. The two other hands departed after a short compliment. Lawrence, however, dawdled, leaving Jon to wonder if he was waiting for him to depart first. A chaperon, perhaps? Had Lawrence actually sensed something between him and Sylvie in the barn?

Rising, Jon grabbed his dishes. When he reached the sink, Sylvie spoke. "I'll do up the dishes later."

He shrugged. "I don't mind doing them."

"I think you've done enough already." Her cold tone made him turn to face her.

"That's right," she said. "I'm not talking about all the fencing you mended, either. I'm talking about acting like my nursemaid. I don't need one."

He set his dishes on the counter and rode out the storm her confrontational attitude caused in him. "I think you do. The sooner you admit that you can't do everything you've done before, at least until the baby is born, the better it will be for both you *and* the baby."

"It was only going to be a short stint on horseback. I wasn't planning to join the rodeo."

"It wouldn't have been a short ride, or else Lawrence wouldn't have minded you going out there on horseback."

She stood and, grabbing the half-filled sauce bowl, stalked to the counter. "I'm well aware that I'm pregnant. And I'm prepared to give my baby the best care I can. Without your help or Lawrence's or even my father's—" She shut her mouth for a moment. "Without anyone's help. Just as I can do these damn dishes without help, as well!"

Her outburst caught Lawrence's interest and he stood. "That's our cue to leave, Jon, my boy. Don't you have some settling in to do?"

Jon heard him, but focused on Sylvie. Hormones. It had to be pregnancy hormones for her to become so rattled, so refusing to accept help.

This wasn't the woman Rick had described to him. Nor was this the kind of sweet, gentle woman his brother would no doubt make love to.

A burst of surprising pride hit him. Rick had made love to this woman. Had pinned her down and impregnated her. Their lovemaking had to have been regular. And protected some of the time. An efficient, career soldier like Sylvie would plan her own pregnancy.

He gritted his teeth. Hot on the heels of the sibling pride was another heated emotion, but he refused to allow it to surface. Instead he focused on Sylvie's pinkened cheeks and bright, flashing eyes.

Somewhere in that tumultuous, defensive mother-to-be was the woman Rick had loved. Jon would simply have to wait for her to appear.

When that gentle woman showed herself, he'd be ready to persuade the truth out of her.

Settling in didn't take long. Once his summer arrangements were made, Jon pulled from his car what he'd bought and packed. On top of the pile he'd just carried in was the new Stetson.

For a bunkhouse, it wasn't what he expected. There was a large, comfortable TV room, heated in the winter by a wood stove. Along a short hallway were four small bedrooms and a bathroom. Austere by his Torontonian standards, but not too shabby.

"What's that smell?" From in front of the TV, Purley lifted his nose to the ceiling and sniffed. "Is that the stink of a new Stetson?"

At the edge of the sofa, and still carrying his luggage, Jon shrugged. He hadn't expected his added presence to go unnoticed, but considering his comments at the supper table, he figured he'd get the cold shoulder from the other men.

He offered a friendly smile. "Sorry about the smell, boys."

"Don't let Sylvie catch a whiff of that hat at breakfast. Might set off some morning sickness."

Michael looked up from the TV. "Might do it some good to get thrown up on, eh, Purley? Break it in and all."

"Coffee."

Everyone turned to face Lawrence. He was sitting at the small table near the woodstove, reading. He lifted the book. It was the father and pregnancy one. "Says here coffee is most likely to send a pregnant woman running to the toilet. And not just to pee."

Purley twisted around. "Hope you're not suggesting we forfeit our coffee. What else does it say?"

"Says that a woman is usually calmer when pregnant."

Purley turned back to watch TV, chuckling. "That's true. Sylvie would have never agreed to take the ATV instead of a horse. We all know that."

Jon frowned. He didn't know that, and quite frankly he didn't find Sylvie calm at all.

"She's gonna look mighty cute all fattened up," Purley continued. "She was always pretty, but she'll be right sweet all swelled up like an udder at sundown."

No wonder Sylvie had so eagerly offered the bunkhouse. Bristling at her craftiness, Jon dropped off his stuff in his room and grabbed his Stetson. He needed some air.

Outside, his gaze automatically gravitated toward the house. One window at the far end glowed, the future nursery, and he watched it, holding his breath.

Over the sounds of the night, and Purley's muffled laugh at the sitcom he was watching, Jon waited.

The scents of campfires and barbecues wound their way from the campground. No fire ban yet for this dry province. A small dog yipped and howled somewhere by the trailer sites.

And still he stared at the window.

Sylvie appeared briefly to shut the curtains and, a moment later, to switch off the light.

Jon rubbed his face. Hell, what was he doing? Waiting for a glimpse of her?

One potent sexual moment hours ago and he was mooning like a teenager? She was carrying his brother's baby, for crying out loud. She'd been his brother's lover.

Again he tried to make some sense of Rick's relationship with her. His brother had respect for her, noting in his e-mails that she was a good supervisor, someone who'd go to bat, all the way if necessary, to see justice done for her subordinates. Not a hint of any budding or covert romance.

In his chest Jon's heart squeezed tight, pushing some hard lump up into his throat. Normally he'd respect Sylvie's privacy, but hell, his brother was dead.

And not once had Rick even hinted to Jon anything about being intimate with Sylvie. Damn strange.

Anger bubbled up, hot and well justified in the cop and older brother part of him. He couldn't ask Rick anymore—

The kitchen light flicked on and Jon caught a glimpse of Sylvie walking around the table.

Rick was dead. The words hurt, even if he couldn't form them on his lips. Suddenly the need to keep his memory alive became more important than Sylvie's privacy. She was with Rick when he died.

And it was about time she told him what really happened that night.

Chapter 6

Sylvie wrapped Marg's apron around her. Too bad that brief nap had to screw up her sleep. But at least she could do some cleaning, though there wasn't much to do. It was too late in the day to do anything else. The endless paperwork that came with running a ranch and a campground didn't appeal to her. She needed to release some of this restless energy.

Besides, the refrigerator could get sorted out. A rare moment, indeed, she considered grimly. Nesting instinct, perhaps?

Throwing open its door, she studied the refrigerator's contents. Among other things, there were two open jars of pickles, three kinds of jam and several near-empty sauce bottles that she was sure she could combine.

The distraction was perfect. No thinking required. She could focus on combining pickles, mixing jams and inventing new barbecue sauces…and not Rick. Or the injustice she and the military had heaped on him. There wasn't anything she could do to help him anymore. And the baby would be fine for the time being. All she had to worry about was herself, and she refused to do that tonight, not with this overloaded refrigerator wrestling for her attention.

"Insomnia or nesting?"

She leaped away from the open door, dropping the squeeze bottle of sauce as she whirled around. "Holy—" Seeing Jon, she caught her expletive. "That's the second time today you've scared the daylights out of me. I suggest a pair of cowboy boots for you. With metal heels."

Jon glanced down at his sneakers. "Sorry. I saw the light on and wondered if you needed anything."

Scooping up the bottle, she tried to calm her racing heart with a fortifying breath. Like her, dark circles had begun to settle under his eyes, giving him a tired, haggard look. He'd had a few sleepless nights himself.

She returned to her task, refusing to allow sympathy to seep in. She'd relent, burst out, maybe even blubber forth a stream of tears of all she'd really done and expect sympathy back. There wouldn't be any. God, no, she'd be a fool to think that. "I've done the dishes and was thinking about cleaning this fridge."

"I can help."

She opened her mouth to protest, but he held up his hand. "Before you kick me out, let me say something. I'm all settled in, but I can't just sit around doing nothing. Lawrence is reading one of his baby books and Purley and Michael are watching TV while making sarcastic remarks about my new Stetson. I know you don't need it, but I'd like to help. Please?"

She shut her mouth. Well, didn't that seem genuine? True, Lawrence preferred to read instead of watching TV, and Purley could keep up the acerbic remarks until the cows came home, so maybe Jon did want to help her. The genuine ring to his voice was a nice change to the anger he'd directed her way. Could he want the company? Could he be lonely, thinking of Rick and automatically seeking his one connection to his dead brother?

Sympathy washed through her, surprising her with its intensity. She could relate to Jon's loneliness. "Sure. Why not?"

He took the items she passed him and began to stack them on the table. Each time she handed him another jar, she felt the brush of his fingertips. Each touch drew out some tiny arc of electricity. Dry air. Nothing more.

"So, do you think you'll miss your work this summer?" she asked him.

He stopped, his hand outstretched and still holding a bottle of lemon juice. Looking thoughtful, he nodded slowly. "T.O. in August is miserable, but yes, I'll miss it."

"I'm surprised. Everyone looks forward to summer vacation."

He set the bottle beside a large container of milk. "Lately I've spent my vacations working with some kids at the local youth center. We hang out, tinker with some dirt bikes, play pool. The kids like that." Lit only by the light from the refrigerator, his expression turned wistful.

"Mentoring?"

"The kids don't like to call it that, but yes, mentoring."

His dark eyes warmed and softened when she nodded.

"But they like it just the same. In Bosnia, a number of platoons, including ours, pitched in to fix up a school and playground. The kids got really excited. So many have lost fathers. Mothers, too." A poignant memory returned. "The language barrier didn't matter. I remember we played soccer with them once. They ran circles around us.''

''I bet that didn't matter, either.''

''Nope.'' Despite the cool air radiating from the open refrigerator, Sylvie felt warm. And a little guilty she was taking Jon from such noble work. ''Makes you feel good, doesn't it?''

''It helps the kids. That's what matters.''

Such integrity deserved to be rewarded, she thought.

Unwilling to let that idea mature, she pulled out the largest container, but it jammed under the wire shelf above it. With her wrist, she tried to shove the shelf up, but the whole awkwardness of the movement made the task impossible.

''Here.'' He leaned over her, his arm extended in front of her as he lifted the upper shelf. All she could see was a wide bicep and the dark dusting of hair on his arm. The sleeve of his plain T-shirt strained over his muscles.

Strong arms. They could easily be her Achilles' heel. Strong, capable arms that could wrap around her when she needed them the most.

She shut her eyes and pulled hard on the deep bowl. It gave, and she stumbled backward. The bowl hit the door shelf and dropped.

One of those strong arms caught her before she could bump to the floor. ''Whoa. All right?''

She blinked up at him, finding only concern in his now warm blue eyes. Tearing away her gaze, she peered down. Between their feet, the bowl rattled and spun like a dying top, the red sauce inside swirling around the transparent lid in a wild Spirograph design.

Jon's palm splayed over her back, lowering her gently to the sitting position. Cradling her in warmth.

''Thanks. I shouldn't have been so impatient.'' Her

words sounded stilted and foolish to her ears, and as much as she wanted to, she couldn't seem to steady herself.

Finally she grabbed the door and tried to pull herself out of his arms. He didn't let go. "No."

Her heart pounding in her chest, she wondered if he'd spoken the word or had she imagined it? A part of her wanted to tell him she was fine and it was all right to let her go, but his arms felt so good around her. Tight, firm, trustworthy.

It seemed so foolish to be sitting here, in his arms, battling the urge to simply stay there forever. She reached out with her right hand and laid her flat palm against his warm chest. Concern deepened in his eyes as he searched her face. Her lips parted when she felt—yes, felt—his gaze settle on her mouth.

What would his lips feel like on hers? As warm as his arms? Warmer than his chest? Would his kiss overpower her like his arms seemed to be doing right now?

"Sylvie?"

He said her name again, all long and smooth like her only silk nightgown, the one she just realized she'd been saving for some special occasion that would never come. She was pregnant, unmarried, looking forward to life as a single mother. Who'd want a knocked-up old soldier with a bad attitude?

Finally she whispered, "Yes?"

He pressed his lips into a tight line, and she forced her gaze back into his eyes. He still held her, a bit more firmly now, and his brows crinkled together slightly. Was he also thinking of how her lips would feel?

"Sylvie, tell me about Rick. What was he doing when he died?"

A sluice of cold doused her foolish ideas. She tried to

push herself free of him, but as if expecting her reaction, he held her tight.

She stiffened. "Is that what you call wanting to help? I don't really appreciate the ulterior motive. But I guess it's not unexpected. Are you going to ask me about Rick each time we're alone? Or just when I'm in your arms?"

"Sylvie, it's a valid question—"

"It'll certainly be at those prenatal classes, too, won't it? I'm practicing my breathing, you're pumping me for information on your brother."

He pulled her back into a tighter embrace, as anger flared in his eyes. To think she'd admired them a moment ago.

"Nice of you to think I'd be that crass. How about I promise you I'll be a perfect gentleman during the classes, if you tell me, right now, how Rick died? Don't you think I deserve to know?"

She tried to twist herself out of his embrace. "I told you I can't say anything more. Even after the investigation is complete. You're a cop. You should know that." She bit her lip and frowned. "Let go of me, please."

He released her, guiding her up to ensure she'd caught her balance.

She straightened her shirt and flicked back an annoying strand of hair. Oh, she should just blurt out everything to him. It wasn't fair and she didn't care for the injustice, but...

But what would Jon say if he knew the truth? From the one decision her captain had made that night to the damn incorrect grid reference and straight to the unexpected ambush. Then on to what she and Rick had done later—the truth wasn't something to be proud of. Even Jon, who so obviously loved his brother, might be ashamed.

Everything had been working against them that night, everything from her captain's decision to send her, right to the miserable, horrible weather.

But still, she had to say something to him. "Jon, you already know everything there is to know. We were ambushed. Rick was shot. He died shortly after. The military isn't keeping anything from you that would give you any more closure. Rick's dead.'' She struggled with her words. "Please bury him."

His expression darkened. "I did. Much later than I should have. I met my brother's body and his escort at the air base in Ottawa, only to find out it was scheduled to be autopsied and I'd have to wait another long, blasted week. I attended the memorial for him at your home unit. Damn it, Sylvie, it wasn't enough!"

"Well, it's just going to have to be!" She spun around and began to yank the rest of the items from the refrigerator, more determined than ever to finish this idiotic, useless task.

Her hands shook. *Do something. Keep busy, don't think of how you'd asked to be Rick's final escort, only to be turned down.*

They refused her. An escort had to be the same rank as the deceased. And she still had to be interviewed. She had the company stores to run. She was needed elsewhere. Those and all the other excuses they'd piled on her just weren't good enough, but she'd had no choice but to accept them.

Jon would have to do the same with her answer.

She plowed past him on her route to the sink with a bowl of something she couldn't recognize, determined to throw it out. Throw it all out. Every last bit of food that had been in the damn refrigerator for more than a day.

And sometime during those determined trips, Jon slipped back outside.

Alone finally, she sank down in front of the refrigerator and let the tears stream down her face. What she wouldn't do to let everything out and get this crying jag over and done with.

Forever.

Nesting. Hormones. Grief. Pregnancy. All the possible reasons for Sylvie's angry cleaning spurt spun around inside Jon's head, slipping past the pain and frustration he still battled.

He was sure she knew way more about Rick's last hours than she was telling. Although, as much as he hated to admit it, strong-arming her wasn't going to induce her to reveal it all. But he refused to wait for the final watered-down military report. Of course he wouldn't be told the truth. Did they think he was stupid? Rick's CO and the Padre and that liaison officer, Major Tirouski, who'd been assigned to the investigation, all assumed he would accept their well-filtered version when they were ready to give it to him.

Jon stopped halfway to the bunkhouse. Turning, he could see Sylvie in the kitchen window, viciously scraping the contents of some bowl into the small compost bin beside the sink.

He would have to be more patient. He *should* be more patient. Sylvie had lost someone dear to her, and she had the right to grieve as well.

Not for the first time, he considered Rick and Sylvie. Together. Lovers. A strange pair, he mulled, his stomach tightening with suspicion. Where did they see their relationship going after Bosnia? She'd been his boss. Even in today's liberated, Ombudsman-filled military, eye-

brows would have lifted at an older supervisor bedding
her subordinate.

Damn, that term didn't sit well with him. Nor did the
police-inspired impression that something more was going on.

He pushed the gut feelings away. He should concen-
trate on discovering the truth about Rick's death. And
ignore the unsettling vision of Rick and Sylvie, oddly
paired lovers.

When he'd pulled her in tight, he knew in a blinding
flash why Rick had been attracted to her. She had the
kind of lean, strong muscles that, when held, melted into
an arousing pliancy he hadn't expected. Add that to her
eyes, as wary and innocent as a deer's, the way her lips
parted and that tempting tongue moistened them, and he
knew exactly what had lured Rick to her.

Then, as he began to fully grasp the attraction, another
blinding truth glared out at him.

She was Rick's, and Jon didn't steal other men's
women, like that bastard had done with his wife.

So what the hell was he doing in her house, cradling
her in his arms, getting his life and emotions all wrapped
around her, a woman who carried another man's baby?

"Just for the summer," he muttered out loud.

But as he moved toward the bunkhouse, the words hit
the night breeze and slapped him back insolently.

The screen door slammed shut and Sylvie looked up
from her ledger book to see who'd entered the campground office. Tuesday mornings were usually quiet.

A man in a combat uniform stood there, peeling off
his sunglasses and beret in one brisk, smooth movement.
She flicked her gaze down to the rank on his shoulders.

Major. The sewn-on name tag announced his name. Tirouski.

"Warrant Officer Mitchell?"

She closed her ledger book. "I'm just Sylvie Mitchell now, Major."

"Warrant Mitchell," he continued, as if her correction had never happened. "My name is Major Tirouski. I'm the liaison officer assigned to the committee investigating Private Cahill's death."

She clenched her jaw. What did they expect to discover that they didn't already know? That the outpost had been relocated, but the information on the new location hadn't been disseminated? That Ops section had given out the wrong grid reference and sent two innocent soldiers into the mountains to get ambushed?

Or would they discover some patsy on whom they could dump all the blame. Like her.

She stood up, as tall as she could manage. "I've already given my statement to the military police. There isn't anything more I can contribute to the investigation."

"The committee has a copy of your statement." He walked up to the counter and perused the office. "So, how's civilian life?"

Not really in the mood for chitchat, nor able to afford the time for any, she stared hard at him. "As you can see, I'm busy. This is a hectic time of year."

She hadn't expected the major to be intimidated by her, and he didn't disappoint her.

He nodded. "Then, Warrant Mitchell, I'll be brief and on my way. One of the reasons we do an investigation of this nature is to help families find some kind of closure. Private Cahill had a brother."

"Yes, I know." When he added nothing, she rolled

her eyes. "And we both know he's here working for me. Has been for just over two weeks. So, who told you?"

"He called and left a voice message telling me where he would be for the summer." The major leaned forward. "We had hoped your captain or perhaps your regimental sergeant-major might have been able to accompany me here, but you realize that they remained in Bosnia to assist with the handover to the next unit. They're still there."

The subtle accusation of desertion floated just beneath the surface. "Why would you want them to come here with you? The RSM already told me I should have stayed in the military for another fifteen years, the way he has."

"So why did you retire?"

A loaded question. "My retirement was already slated before I went to Bosnia. The early-release incentives were too attractive." At least she could say that truthfully, even though the decision had turned out to be a bigger blessing than she'd planned. She'd given her statement at the start of the investigation, then asked her CO to repatriate her sooner than scheduled.

The word *desertion* had hovered around her all the way home. For a moment she had clear insight as to why Tirouski was really here, and the anger and guilt inside of her flared again. Yes, she'd gotten Rick killed, as good as killed him herself, but the whole awful night had started with the military's mistake, and now this major was here to make sure those mistakes were damn well kept hidden.

That was his only reason for being here.

The major glanced around the office. "Is Constable Cahill around?"

Jon and Lawrence were at the far end of the ranch, and though hardly an hour's ride away, she was glad they weren't planning to return for lunch. "I believe he's at the north corner. And quite unavailable." She leaned to her right and spotted the gray staff car through the window. "You won't be able to drive out in that. Can I give him a message for you? Have you completed the investigation?"

"Nearly. But it's not Constable Cahill I'm here to see. It's you."

She narrowed her eyes and waited for him to elaborate.

"As you are aware, Warrant, the investigation is covering some sensitive issues, militarily speaking, that is. Of course we hope to discover who ambushed you, and make some recommendations for protocol changes."

Right, yeah. And all because one private died in the line of duty? The only thing that concerned them was if the media got wind of their mistake, not that one private died in a theater of operation that usually saw a ten-percent fatality rate. She gritted her teeth. "The only protocol that needs to be changed is to teach certain people how to read a map."

The major bristled. "I believe you have already been briefed on how we are proceeding—"

"Sweeping under the rug, you mean." Sylvie drew in her breath. "Ops should look at who they're trusting these days. A man died after we'd been given the wrong directions." *Even though I killed him with a mistake of my own.* Despite her unspoken admission, she returned Tirouski's hard stare.

"That is none of your concern, Warrant Officer Mitchell." His words cut through his tight lips.

"I'm not a warrant officer anymore, Major."

"You are still on terminal leave, are you not?"

"Yes."

"And so, *Warrant Officer Mitchell,*" he emphasized

her name and rank, "you are still subject to the Code of Service Discipline. That includes keeping sensitive information to yourself."

Finally he'd stopped beating around the bush. Someone at HQ had realized where Jonathan Cahill had gone for the summer and was starting to sweat. Hmm, could they trust Mitchell to keep her mouth shut?

Yes, oh yes, but she wasn't about to allow this major to pull rank on her. "Major Tirouski, Jonathan Cahill came looking for closure and I needed help for the summer."

"He's a police officer. He doesn't need a job."

"No. What he needs is to deal with his brother's death in his own way, and if that means working long, hard hours chasing cattle on *my* ranch, then who are you to say he shouldn't be here? And we both know that I signed a nondisclosure form in Bosnia stating I wouldn't discuss Rick's death." She leaned over the counter and found herself practically bumping noses with the man. "Well, I haven't. Nor do I plan to."

Six months ago she'd never have pulled such insubordination, but she no longer had her career to worry about. On the line today was her privacy. And Jon's.

And the privacy of her tiny baby, whose existence was temporarily hidden by a high countertop.

The major straightened, pulling from an inner pocket a photocopied document. "Just to refresh your memory, Warrant."

He handed the paper to her, but she didn't need to read the form again. Her pulse pounded in her throat.

"Under the provisions of the Official Secrets Act, you may not disclose any information, period, whether you consider what happened a mistake or not. If you do, Warrant, you can be charged under the Code of Service Discipline, with a court martial, as you are still in the service, technically.''

He pulled out his beret and fitted it to his head. Then, still watching her face, he slipped on his sunglasses. The cool eyes disappeared. ''And that code hasn't become any more lenient since you retired.''

''Breathe in slowly, slowly, hold it, and…exhale. Make each exhalation as long as the inhalation. Focus on the breath, not the pain.''

Sitting cross-legged on the floor of the birthing center's family room, Sylvie drew in as much air as her lungs would allow. As the public health nurse said, she focused on the breath.

Better than focusing on the events of this morning, and how she'd stewed all day at the major's not-so-subtle warning.

Mind you, she thought as she let out a long, controlled exhalation, she wasn't sure she could focus on her breathing as long as Jon's arm supported her back, either. And what about the dark head just inches from her face, so close that if she were to turn around, she'd be only a heartbeat from a kiss?

Jon. He knew nothing of Major Tirouski's visit, and she more than hoped to keep it that way. Even now, the shame of her act and the anger that the military had backed her into a corner made it hard to think.

Focus. Breathe out. She let out her inhalation in a long, measured length, trying to match her breathing to the heavily pregnant woman's on the next mat. Tirouski had come as close as possible to openly threatening her today. Sylvie stifled a dry laugh. He'd wasted his time driving all the way down to see her. She'd signed the gag order. Nothing would make her go back on her word.

Jon shifted beside her, no doubt attempting to get more comfortable on the thin gymnastics mat. She steeled herself as he ducked his head once, sending her way a waft of some warm, spicy scent from his evening shower.

She shut her eyes. He smelled so good.

"If it's too hard to kneel beside me, go sit down," she whispered between breaths while restraining the urge to clear her throat of his enticing scent.

"I'm comfortable. How about you?"

Hardly. Not with him so close. It couldn't be attraction, even as handsome as Jon was. He was Rick's brother, a man who wanted two things from her. The truth about Rick's death and a chance to know his nephew or niece.

She drew in another long, focusing breath. Forget him. He may get the latter, but he'll never get the former.

The nurse called out, "Breathe, ladies. In…and…out. Dads, help our mums."

Jon shifted closer to her, and his breath danced across her warm face. Did they have to keep this place so damn hot? He leaned in toward her and rubbed a maddeningly distracting circle between her aching shoulder blades. "Breathe, Sylvie," he mimicked the nurse quietly.

She let a long seethe. "If I have to do anymore damn deep breathing, I'll turn into a Hindu monk."

He snickered in her ear, and the sound dissolved deliciously through her like the first morsel of one of Marg's brownies, still warm from the oven. She'd deliberately avoided Jon ever since that night in the kitchen, more than two weeks ago. She hadn't gone out to inspect the line shack, either, for fear of running into him.

He'd shown his true colors that night. She'd been tempted to fire him on the spot, but that would leave her so desperately short-handed.

"Okay, Mums," the nurse called out, "let's get you

on your sides. Dads, we're going to run through some simple massage techniques. If your wife's back doesn't ache now, you can be sure it will.''

During the communal chuckling, Sylvie did as the nurse instructed. She lay on her side, facing away from Jon, tensing, waiting for his firm fingers to knead into the tired muscles of her lower back.

The nurse chatted on, and Jon followed her cheerful instructions.

Oh, his fingers were heaven on earth. Sylvie clamped her eyes shut, afraid someone in the room, anyone, really, would see how much his touch affected her. How much his warm fingers could make her forget Tirouski's offending visit.

Behind her, Jon drew in a long breath and worked deeper into the thick, knotted muscles on either side of her spine. She let out a quiet groan, not realizing until that minute how much she truly ached.

''Feel good?''

She nodded. ''I hadn't realized how much I needed this.''

''That's because you've been ignoring your body.''

Her eyes flew open. Was she that transparent? ''I've got too much to do to pamper this pregnancy. And besides, if all your body did was throw up and dump an elephant on your back, you'd try to ignore your pregnancy, as well.''

He leaned forward, digging his knuckles deep into one tense spot and making her eyes widen and water with the exquisite pain. ''I guess I'll never know. Except, of course, if I listen to Lawrence.''

She stifled an unexpected giggle. ''What's he been doing lately?''

''Reading out loud what we all can expect. Of course,

we're all banned from looking at the photos, especially Purley.''

She burst out laughing, causing several other parents-to-be to glance their way. ''Purley used to be married. He's been divorced for about twenty years now. I figured Michael would have been more interested. He's younger, hasn't had a date since the spring and, like Lawrence, has never married. Oh, yes, there!''

He worked the knot. ''Maybe they don't know what they're missing.''

''Well, those pictures can't be very exciting.''

Jon leaned forward again. She caught his soft chuckle as it danced past her ear. ''You'd be surprised what a man finds exciting. And at the worst times.''

Huh?

When she blinked, a vision that shouldn't be imagined waltzed through her mind. She shut her eyes, trying to force the unseemly erotic image away. But it lingered, defiant like the man who dominated it. A man with dark hair and strong hands and a lean frame that could cover a woman's in one fluid, purposeful thrust.

Abruptly another man's face slashed over her.

No! Please, no. Rick was dead. Dead because of her stupid poor judgment.

Go away!

Something caught in her throat, hard enough to choke her.

Oh, hell. Tears sprang into her eyes from nowhere. Not just a few, either. Within the second, they streamed down her face, and the same knot of fear and terror from that night tightened in her chest, cutting off what little breathing she could manage.

Why did she do it? Why couldn't she have used a bit

more common sense, stopped everything they'd done before it all started?

Stuck along a road they shouldn't have been on, miles from their only aid....

Oh, no! Not here! Sobs jammed between her shoulders, then pounded up her throat in brutal rhythm with her heart. Jon immediately stopped his massage.

He leaned over her. "Sylvie? What—"

She pulled away from him and struggled to stand up. The nurse stopped her instruction, and Sylvie cast a blurred, terrified glance around at the other curious parents before racing from the room.

Chapter 7

Jon found her outside, and his sigh of relief came all the way from his feet. Thank God she was still here.

With the sun having finally set, only security lights lit the lawn behind the clinic. Their cool circles didn't quite reach Sylvie out there on the picnic table, but he recognized her form immediately. She was crying, her shoulders pumping up and down.

"Sylvie?"

She stopped but didn't turn around. She stayed seated on the table, her feet firmly planted on the bench. He said nothing more, just climbed up beside her.

When her crying resumed, he pulled her into his arms, holding her firmly against him, refusing to let her rigid body go. Too bad if she didn't want him to embrace her. She needed it right now.

"Damn him."

He loosened his grip and peered down at her. "Who?"

"Why us? We had nothing and he knew it, but he still let us drive into an ambush!"

He could barely understand her sobbing, jumbled words. She turned in his arms and he could see her face contorted with frustration as she continued, "Hell, it was so stupid! I didn't care who that guy sympathized with. He knew it would have been a waste of time to ambush us. It made no sense! He could have changed everything if he'd just paid attention to our manifest!"

Still clinging to her, Jon struggled to understand her words. What made no sense? Who was she talking about? Changed everything?

Like Rick's death?

He held his breath, hoping she might elaborate. Praying silently that she'd tell him more.

But she didn't. And as much as the temptation to pump her for more information burned him, he held back. She was blaming someone for something, a decision that had resulted in Rick's death?

Damn.

He blinked. *Tell me more, Sylvie. Please.*

But for too many long, anguished minutes, they sat there, silently listening to the sounds of the night. A car horn somewhere. Inside the clinic a baby wailed, loud and long enough to penetrate the insulated walls. Crickets joined the chorus of noise.

But she stayed silent in his arms. Damn. Suppressing his disappointment, he finally asked, "Ready to go home?"

She pulled away, sniffing. "Sorry about that."

He froze when his feet reached the ground. Adrenaline surged through him. About what? Her display? Or revealing something she shouldn't have?

No, he wouldn't ask her about it. By giving her space

the past few weeks and letting her warm up to him, he'd managed to get more info than any of his strong-arm tactics had. Someone was to blame. He tried an ineffectual shrug. "Lawrence would say it's hormones."

She looked up at him. The security lights caught that innocent look again. "Don't tell anyone, okay? It *is* just hormones. Plus, I...I guess I'm more tired than I figured. And the stress of retiring. I didn't get a SCAN."

"A scan?"

"It stands for Second Career Assistant Network. It's a series of lectures and workshops designed to help you readjust to civilian life. All that bawling is the stress of retiring working itself out." She stood up and straightened her shoulders.

Like hell it was just the stress of retiring. Didn't she even remember what she'd just wailed?

Maybe not. Sometimes during stressful situations, a person pushed certain memories away. He took her hand and helped her off the picnic table. "Why don't you sleep in tomorrow? Or even for the next few days? We guys can fend for ourselves. It won't kill us. Though my omelettes might."

She smiled. "I'd love to, but I haven't yet been out to the line shack. I need to get that sorted out. If there's some way it can be salvaged—"

"It's waited this long for you. Let me do it. I won't be able to go there for a few days, but it certainly isn't beyond my capabilities."

"No. I need to know the full extent of the damage. We use that shack in the fall and winter, not to mention it's near the water pump. If it has to be rebuilt, then it's my responsibility. I'll have to find the money somewhere—"

Still holding her hand, he shook his head. "Nothing's

going to change tonight, or even during the next few days. If you want to go out there, that's fine. Just not tomorrow or the day after, okay? Don't worry about it. It's probably not as bad as Lawrence claims.''

She nodded. He released her hand and they began to walk around the center. Halfway around, he found himself wanting to end the heavy silence between them. ''I'll look at the shack, and if it's as bad as Lawrence says, I'll radio you. You can call the carpenter right away.''

She peered at him, and the sense of innocent victim returned. And again the question he didn't want to answer arose. Did he have the right to interrogate her? Could he treat his brother's lover so harshly?

Damn but he wasn't sure of anything anymore.

Putting his back to the early-morning sun, Jon shook his head in disgust. His two-way radio. At least he'd found his two-way radio. He hadn't spoken much to Sylvie these past few days, not since that fateful prenatal class. But that would have to change.

Normally the radios sat on the kitchen counter overnight, charging, but when he went for his, radio number five, it was missing.

Not anymore.

Ground into the dirt path that led from the office to the trailer sites, and pulverized by several forward and backward trips of some vehicle, there wasn't much left of it to recognize, except for a shard of the plastic casing that must have flung out when the tire first ran over it. The shard bore the sticker number five.

Vandals. Maybe those teenagers who liked to hang around the petting zoo after dark. If she didn't already do so, Sylvie would have to start locking her back door at night. Whether or not she felt it was necessary. It would be a wise precaution any way one looked at it.

Maybe the men could take turns sleeping on the cot in the small room off the kitchen.

Yeah, like Sylvie would go for that. Ever since the incident at the prenatal class, she'd kept clear of everyone, especially him. Had she realized she'd blurted out too much, and feared he would confront her for more?

Or did she fear that he'd demand the truth from the review committee set up to investigate Rick's death, asking who had access to the truck's manifest, and who knew where they were going.

Working his jaw, he peered down at the shard in his hand. He should demand answers from that committee. All they'd done was send a letter informing him of the impending investigation. And not a damn peep since. Not even from that liaison, Major Tirouski.

Sighing, Jon stooped and gathered up the broken neon green fragments of the radio, all the while committing to memory the design of the tire tracks that surrounded them. A wide tire, with deeply grooved tracks. Too bad he couldn't take a plaster cast.

When he looked up, he spied Sylvie walking to the house, her right hand occasionally dropping to her now slightly swollen belly. He should tell her about this.

His insides clenched. But he doubted she'd take the advice he'd offer. Strong-arming the truth about Rick hadn't worked, so why expect her to do something about a little vandalism? She'd blame it on teenagers.

No, he'd have to find the right moment before he spoke.

Sylvie spotted the dangerous lean to the building while still on the far crest. No wonder Lawrence wanted it torn down.

She could also see Jon, swinging his leg wide as he dismounted Stampede, a big gelding, called so because he had lived up to his name at a very early age.

She hadn't talked to Jon since last week at her prenatal classes. She'd seen him only at meals. And until this minute she'd kept every scrap of what had happened that evening shoved in a dark, well-hidden corner of her mind.

Now, slowing down the ATV, she tried to relive those lamenting moments outside the clinic…tried to pull back into the light what she'd said and done.

But…but she couldn't. Oh, Lord, she drew a blank. What had she said? She'd blubbered on and on after realizing she couldn't hold back the tears any longer.

All that lingered now could only be described as a bad blur, like those nightmares of hers where the memories of the emotions clung to her damp body long after she'd woken. Jon had casually joked about how easily a man could be aroused, and suddenly she'd fallen apart. When her tears had run out, he had taken her home. And said nothing.

Everything seemed confusing, out of her grasp. Yet, his little joke ran like a broken record through her head. Were any of those emotions for him? Even now, with only the aftertaste swimming inside of her, an unwelcomed, heady swell of something tried to choke out all of her other feelings.

She quickly adjusted her helmet. What she'd said last week at prenatal class would have to wait. Ahead, Jon and Lawrence waited beside their mounts, watching her approach. It couldn't have been bad, because Jon remained calm and cordial to her. Right?

She clenched her jaw. With deliberate focus, she

turned her attention to the half-dilapidated shack beside the two men.

Deep breath. In, two, three, out, two, three.

It worked. Well, surprise, surprise. Repeating the breathing actually helped. She pulled up several yards away from the men, leaving the engine to idle.

"That thing give you any trouble?" Lawrence asked, nodding to the ATV.

She pulled off her helmet and fluffed her hair. "It was hard to start, that's all. We'll take it in for a tune-up next week."

"I'll have a look at it," Jon volunteered. "Save your money for this building."

She looked over at Jon, again thankful he'd convinced her to sleep in this past week. And, judging from Lawrence's casual behavior, Jon hadn't mentioned her shameful outburst. She smiled grimly at him. "Thanks."

They quickly surveyed the shack, Sylvie cataloging the damage on a notepad she'd brought with her.

"The foundation's still good. Looks like it's been torn from away on this side," Lawrence said, walking around.

Starting to follow, Sylvie slipped past Jon, who waited for her to walk ahead. His eyes, shielded by the brim of his new Stetson, looked dark, disapproving, as if something about her disturbed him.

She caught up with Lawrence, all too aware of Jon's big frame close behind. He'd wrapped his arms around her while she'd sobbed, and though the painful emotions, in lieu of memories, lingered still, they were amazingly tempered by a warmth. His warmth.

"See here?" Lawrence bent down and pointed to where the wood had torn from its slab foundation.

Sylvie nodded. "I remember when Dad built this. He

figured the concrete foundation would help it last longer.''

"Looks like it's been hit by vandals," Jon said.

Sylvie looked up at Jon in disbelief. "Vandals? Out here?"

"Could be. No matter where you go, there's always a chance of vandalism." He folded his arms. "Someone smashed one of the two-way radios. I found it this morning.''

She frowned. "Where?"

"Imbedded in the dirt path between the house and campground. Someone had run over it several times."

She straightened, not wanting to look at him, but hoping that the conversation would stay focused on the building. "This place has been rammed by something, and split most of the wood on this side. But we might be able to salvage it."

Lawrence lifted his brows incredulously. "How?"

"Well," she answered, making a few quick sketches. "In Bosnia most of the buildings are brick, but there was this wooden building the Combat Engineers had put up when they first arrived about ten years ago. It got damaged last fall and ended up looking like this shack." She flicked her pen up to the splintered wall. "I watched them use a couple of come-alongs and a truck to straighten it, then they reinforced it with two-by-fours. Like this." She scribbled out another rough sketch. "Maybe we can do the same thing here."

She looked up from her notepad to Jon, who then glanced over at Lawrence, before settling his gaze back on her. "It could work," he said.

Sylvie folded her arms. Well now, was that admiration in his eyes? Hadn't he figured she could be resourceful?

Yet, despite the tiny spurt of sarcasm rising in her, her cheeks warmed.

Lawrence scrubbed his face. "Yep, I think we might be able to. We could rent the come-alongs and a cement drill at that place in town. The only other alternative is to tear it down."

"Which will happen, anyway, if the straightening doesn't work," she finished for him. "I'd like to attempt to repair it first."

Lawrence walked back to his horse. "And I'd like to finish the fence repairs before that. When do you want to try this?"

Today was Thursday, and if they did try to start right away, it would be Saturday before they could get out here again. Weekends were too busy for the campground part of the business, with Purley spending all his time ferrying hikers out to the trail and back. "I'll set aside the time and let you know."

"Fine by me. If you don't mind, I'll get back to my fences." Lawrence swung up onto his horse and rode away.

Finally Sylvie flipped her notebook closed.

"Feel better today?"

Now a dusty dot to the west, Lawrence had left her alone with Jon. Drawing in a fortifying breath, she turned. "Yes, thank you." She added, "I'm glad I've slept in this past week."

"Perhaps you should make sleeping in a regular thing especially now that you're in your second trimester."

Surprised at his advice, she lifted her eyebrows. "What do you know about second trimesters? Oh, I forgot. Lawrence?"

He smiled. "You really knew what you were doing,

bunking me with those guys. I think I'd rather camp out in a pup tent all summer.''

She allowed herself to feel a little smug. "Information overload?''

"Almost. With not much on TV, we're all set to learn about the third and final trimester.'' He grimaced and shook his head.

"It'll teach you tolerance.''

"Not to mention all about stretch marks, protruding navels and something about Kegel muscles I'd rather not repeat.''

She smiled briefly. Just a smile? What the hell was wrong with her? What was happening to Jon was hilarious. She'd known exactly what she'd been doing when she sent him to the bunkhouse, and yet there was little satisfaction from the comical situation.

Frowning, she started toward the ATV, which still idled nearby.

As she approached, the engine sputtered and died.

She stopped and threw up her hands. "Great. I had trouble earlier. I'll never get it started now.''

"I'll see what I can do. Did I tell you I have a bit of mechanical experience behind me?''

She peeked over her shoulder. "You do?''

"I was top of my shop class in high school.''

She slapped her pad and pen down on the black vinyl seat. "That's it? High school shop? Even I had that.''

Jon leaned against the ATV's rear basket and casually crossed his strong, tanned arms. "With help from a friend of mine on the same shift, I rebuilt some old dirt bikes for a youth rally last year. It gave the inner-city kids a chance to get out and enjoy a bit of legal speed.''

"For a backyard mechanic, you're not doing too much work.'' She had to say something. Just standing there,

Jon exuded a confident sex appeal that simply steamrol-
led over her. So much strength.

Her hand strayed to her stomach. She was pregnant
with his brother's baby, and every night the memories of
those final hours on that winding, muddy road flooded in
on her. And every morning, in the dark, quiet hours before dawn, she fought them back, battling the injustice
with a determination even her military training hadn't
completely forged. Then, as the sun rose, and the strength
inside of her was expended, she found herself drained
and tired.

She didn't need Jon's steamrolling sex appeal to
weaken her further. She might give in to the foolish desire to want him. Or accidentally let slip what really happened to Rick. And, oh God, risk a court martial?

Beside her, Jon still hadn't moved, except to poke his
hat up slightly with a long, tanned forefinger. She eyed
him. "So, tool boy, are you going to do something or
just stand there and look good against that rattletrap?"

With one hand he pushed himself away from the ATV.
Patience he had, for most things, but where Rick was
concerned, it took much, much more effort. In a calm
manner, he'd tried to ease the tension Sylvie constantly
carried. Maybe even see one of her beautiful, lingering
smiles, the ones she doled out by the eyedropper.

He'd chalked up her coolness to the situation she
faced, and didn't expect to ever see her truly, warmly
smile. Shadows under her eyes told him she wasn't getting the rest she needed, despite claiming she appreciated
the opportunity to sleep in.

It had been over a week since she'd discussed Rick
with him. Had she forgotten him so soon? Surely not.
She carried his baby inside of her. Jon spied her just now

resting her hand on her stomach, her expression going pensive a moment.

He turned his attention to the ATV.

The engine abruptly backfired.

Then, in the next instant, without him even feeling it happen, he was on his back beside the ATV, his Stetson rolling away.

Sylvie had sprawled herself over him. Her eyes like saucers, she stared past his head. Automatically his arms wrapped around her.

"Sylvie?"

"Shhh! They're out there! Did you see where they fired from?"

He tilted his head way back, but saw only the quiet pastureland and imposing mountain backdrop, all upside down. And he heard nothing but soft breezes and crickets. And Sylvie's speedy panting. He tightened his arms, pressing her torso closer to his chest. "It's okay, sweetheart."

She jerked her head down, and he knew instantly she didn't see him. There was that innocent wariness again.

Just as he tried to study it, she blinked him into focus again, and offered a wobbly laugh that sounded more like a cough than anything else.

"I'm sorry. I...the ATV backfired?"

"Yes," he answered slowly, searching her face for something he couldn't quite put his finger on. Another memory? Perhaps, but it felt like something else. "The engine backfired. It needs a tune-up, remember?"

With another self-conscious laugh she sagged against him, allowing her forehead to drop to his shoulder. "I guess my nerves are shot."

Her words branded themselves into his shoulder, her breath too warm, too noticeable. She fit perfectly against him. He wanted to grind himself into the soft flesh of her abdomen, but against his growing arousal pressed a rounded reminder of her condition.

Damn, she was filling out. Her breasts crushed between them, and one glance down was all he needed to sate his mind with her lush cleavage, bigger, fuller than even last week. Need surged through him. He wanted her. All of her, right now, and with a strength that startled him.

Hell, what was he doing? She carried Rick's baby. Hadn't he learned anything from Tanya? Except Tanya had never worn the naive look Sylvie often wore. Or was he just feeding his oversensitive intuition?

To hell with it. He caught the nape of her neck and yanked her head down. His lips found hers with instinctive accuracy.

He forced her mouth open, his tongue inviting itself inside. He watched her reaction, up close and personal, a big part of him praying she wouldn't push him away.

When her eyes drifted shut and her mouth yielded to his tongue, he rolled them both over. There was very little technique in her kiss, but her lips were sweet, willing, open. His hand jammed in under her, scraping against an exposed rock. He ignored it. He tried to insinuate himself between her legs, but they remained tangled like the long, parched grass under them.

He wanted to taste her. All of her. Ignoring the good sense that out here on the wide-open prairie was no place for lovemaking, he abandoned her mouth for the smooth skin of her neck.

Down, down he went, using his lips to force back the loose shoulder of her cotton blouse and taste her swelling breasts. Only when the material resisted, did he lift and turn his head. That and a need for a decent breath.

One of the ATV's thick tires lay in his line of barely focused vision.

And imbedded in the deep grooves of the wide tread were translucent shards of neon green.

His radio?

Someone, driving this ATV, had smashed and run over his radio? Several vicious times, too.

And apart from himself, only Sylvie had been driving this vehicle lately.

He turned his head and found Sylvie watching him, eyes wide and innocent, lips moist and bruised, all of her begging to be kissed again. She'd kissed him with nothing more than passion. No expertise. Total innocence, if that was at all possible in this day and age. And the idea made her look like the finest food to a starving man.

Had she looked so delicious to Rick?

Oh, hell. What was he doing?

He pushed himself off her. "I didn't hurt you, did I?"

She blinked, her expression dazed. "No."

He knelt beside her, watching as she twisted around to a sitting position. He should help her. But, God help him, he couldn't.

A moment ago, he'd managed to overpower his own good sense, and frankly, watching her tug her neckline back into place, covering the marks he'd seared into her pale skin, he knew if he touched her again, he'd finish what he'd started.

Right here in the middle of blasted nowhere.

No. There was something he needed to do first. He jumped up and grabbed the pen she'd set down beside her notepad.

"What are you doing?"

Kneeling again, he pried loose the largest shard of neon plastic. It popped out into the grass, but he found it immediately. Holding it out in his flat palm, he said, "This is a piece of the two-way radio. And as far as I know, beside me, you're the only one to have driven this ATV. Why did you run over it?"

Shame burned into her cheeks. She struggled to stand and, frustrated that her center of balance had changed, she grabbed the utility basket behind the seat to haul herself up.

Jon had already stood by the time she straightened. "Why, Sylvie?"

"It was broken, all right? I couldn't get it to work and it ticked me off. It was nothing personal."

"When did you take it? I usually have it from breakfast every morning until supper. We don't need the radios any other time."

"I borrowed it late one night. Please don't ask me about it. I...I can't tell you why I took it." She couldn't look at him. Her own behavior that night had scared the hell out of her. And now, in the light of day, her actions seemed stupid, illogical. Even she had questioned her damn sanity after the fact.

And in the same way she was questioning, right now, the prudence of kissing Jon.

She must be crazy. What had just happened? How did she go from talking to kissing?

Oh, Lord, she remembered. The sounds of that horrible night in Bosnia still rang clearly in her head. The stream of pops, the terrifying realization they were being fired upon, the way her heart pounded as she'd shoved Rick to the ground and fallen on him.

She'd participated in plenty of exercises using blank ammo, perhaps too many. They don't prepare anyone for the real thing, the scream of the bullet as it whizzes past your ear, the sharp ping where it ricochets off the truck's front bumper, the dread that swells up in one's chest before you even realize it's bullets hailing down on you.

Those damn bullets still rebounded in her head. And she'd driven Jon to the ground and fallen on top of him, protecting him the way she'd done to Rick.

Lord, the parallels went further than just that.

She'd given in to the temptation and kissed Jon.

She'd done the same cowardly thing *that night*. No, worse. Way worse.

Repeating *that* mistake wasn't in the game plan. She wasn't that crazy, no matter how much Jon's kisses heated hidden places in her that shouldn't be heated and weakened her willpower nearly to the point of total stupid submission.

Finally finding her balance, she leaned over the ATV and twisted the ignition key.

The engine rolled over, the high-pitched whine of a small, powerful starter cutting through her. Beyond, Stampede snorted, anxious himself to be moving again.

Nothing. The engine didn't catch. She tried it again, yanking out the manual choke furiously, but pressing her finger and thumb tight against the key didn't make the engine catch any better.

She swore, shoved the choke back in again and tried the starter one more time. Nothing but the insistent whine of an engine not catching one damn bit.

"Sylvie!" Jon's hand closed over hers and she jumped. "Sylvie, stop it. You'll only flood it, and it's still hot enough to backfire again."

She yanked her hand free. With her face still aflame, she grabbed the pen, shoved it into the notepad and stalked away.

"Where are you going?"

She couldn't look at him. Instead she yelled up to the big blue sky. "Home. I'll send Purley out with the truck. Go and help Lawrence."

Thankfully, he didn't try to catch her. What a disaster this trip out here had been. First the engine backfired, driving her to the ground like some nutcase with shell shock. Then she'd given in to Jon's kisses. And it would have been so easy to take those kisses all the way.

She kept on walking.

Then Jon had noticed that plastic shard. Smashing that radio had been a stupid, childish thing to do, something she could never be proud of, or even barely acknowledge. The sooner they both forgot about it, the better off she'd be.

A pounding of hooves warned her he'd mounted Stampede. She stopped dead in her tracks as the big horse raced past and in front of her. Jon hauled in hard on the reins, and the horse skidded to a halt, with a sharp whinny of protest.

Her head still down low, she dared a glance up at him. A few minutes ago they'd been locked in such passion, the mere memory stole her breath. What she wouldn't do to feel his lips on her skin again.

She'd welcomed his primitive male act, as if she were some simple woman bent on her own pleasure.

She'd done that in Bosnia.

Spinning around, she tried to circumvent Jon, but he was too fast. In a move that rivaled his swift decision to kiss her, he leaped down. "Stop."

"No. For crying out loud, I'm walking home."

"It's too far."

"It's not. I'm not an invalid, Jon. Don't pamper me."

He caught her arm. "I'll take you home."

She looked up at him. He'd shoved his Stetson way

back on his head, and the sun beat down on his face, exposing every tiny crevice and line.

He looked older. And sexier and...so intense.

Leftover passion, nothing more. This aborted attempt had left a gaping maw inside of her and was trying to trick her into filling it.

"I'm fine, Jon. It's not that far."

"You can ride Stampede."

She laughed incredulously. "Now, that's a change. Last week you didn't want me riding."

He slid his hand down to hers. She'd have yanked her arm back, but the touch feathered her skin so lightly, she hadn't been sure it had really happened. Saying nothing, he led her back to the horse. "Do you need help mounting?"

Another round of heat burned her cheeks. She'd worked around enough men to hear the sexual innuendo in his words. But a quick glimpse of his face told her the sleazy thought hadn't crossed his mind. "No. I can manage."

She swung up onto Stampede, but it took nearly all her effort. She was out of shape, out of balance and out of willpower to fight.

Just as she gathered up the reins, Jon threw his arm across her lap to grab the saddle horn. The next instant, he swung himself up and over Stampede's rump.

She jumped and shifted her weight to counteract his sudden move. The horse stepped sideways, also shocked by the unexpected extra weight. "What are you doing?"

"Whoa, Stampede," he called over her shoulder to the horse. Then, once he was settled on the bare rump of the big gelding, he wrapped his arms around her. She stiffened immediately.

"Relax. Stampede can handle both of us. And our

combined weight will keep him from acting up and racing home.''

"You don't trust me." Did he have to treat her like a
misbehaving child? "I wouldn't have raced him home."

"I do trust you. It's Stampede I don't trust. And I
could have taken the reins and walked beside you the
entire way, but this is quicker. We don't have all day to
roam the range.''

She turned her head slightly to face him, finding him
so close, she bumped into the rim of his hat. Surely her
burning cheeks stung him with heat? "We found time to
kiss, didn't we?''

A distinct pause. "There's always time for that." He
smiled at her, but now the sun shaded his eyes and she
couldn't tell whether or not he meant what he said or was
just helping to ease her embarrassment.

She faced the front, feeling foolish and childish with
nothing to grip but the horn.

As if reading her mind, he offered her the reins. "Take
them. Just keep him at a walk.''

When she took the reins, Jon's hands settled lightly on
her hips. Her ever-widening hips, she thought with dis-
may. She'd barely had the sense of balance to mount
Stampede.

They said nothing for a while, Sylvie forcing herself
to relax and enjoy the gentle motion, the warmth of both
the sun and Jon and the grateful fact he hadn't pushed
the radio issue.

Why, she could drift off to sleep in Jon's—

Something gentle brushed against her nearly full bladder, a sweeping, inside movement—

She gasped. There it was again.

"What's wrong?"

With a sharp pull on the reins, she stopped Stampede.

Her breath caught in her throat, she whispered. "I felt something. Like a brush along my bladder. Down deep. There!" She turned her head to stare at Jon. She must have looked utterly foolish with her mouth agape and her eyes wide. She grabbed Jon's hand and pressed it against the lowest part of her belly. Not too firmly. She was in perpetual need of peeing. "Can you feel it? The baby's moving!"

She didn't dare breathe, in case the tiny flutter had been her imagination. Deep inside of her, something danced. To her the movement felt like the gentle brush of one of the hungry Bosnian children, one who might dare reach into her truck to touch her arm with skinny fingers. Looking for a handout of the caramels she always carried for them.

Behind her Jon stilled. Even against the constant wind, she could feel his quick inhalation.

The baby gave another flutter under his flat palm. He leaned forward, and pressed his hand more firmly against her belly.

Sylvie melted with a pleasure that swirled through her chest. Life. Beautiful life, growing within her. No wonder the minister at the church where Lawrence had taken her when she returned had spoken of the gift of children. Of sharing a gift with a loved one—

Suddenly the intimacy of the situation struck her hard. She'd seen several moms at the prenatal classes offer their enormous bellies to anyone who wished to feel their unborn moving. It had all seemed natural for them, but she hadn't been able to bring herself to feel a tiny foot or knee or hand.

But now, as the rolling foothills filled the background behind Jon, and his warm body matched the glaring sun, the whole idea of sharing her baby's tiny movements had become shockingly private…and personal.

He drew in another sharp breath and pressed his hand closer in. ''I can't feel it.''

She twisted around farther. Jon had leaned forward, his Stetson pushed back so he didn't bump her with the rim, and she could see the concentration riveting his handsome features and yet at the same time smoothing out those fine lines that splayed away from his eyes. Did he look that way when he was making love? Or was such concentration reserved for the baby, his only connection to his brother?

Her heart squeezed. His tiny nephew or niece moved against Jon's hand one more time, though his look told her he still felt nothing.

He deserved this moment and…she wanted him to have it! More than anything. Whether he could feel the moment or not.

He'd come here for closure, and she knew he wouldn't leave until he got it, in whatever form. She'd hoped he would find it out on the range or helping a stranger's kids feed Andrea's ridiculous pig or maybe on the back of Stampede.

Alone, on the back of Stampede.

She shifted away, and when he glanced down at her face, a quiet, slightly sad smile tugged up the corners of her mouth.

In an odd way, Sylvie realized, Jon was punishing her for Rick's death and her own silence. Telling him the truth might take the heat off her, but she knew he'd never keep it a neat, packaged secret. Never. She'd then face a court martial, a disgraceful end to an otherwise excellent career.

Jon's hand pressed deeper in against her lower belly, while he shifted closer to her.

She was sandwiched in more ways than one.

"Amazing," he said. "According to Lawrence's books, the baby usually doesn't move until it's eighteen or nineteen weeks old. How is it possible so soon?"

"I don't know. I guess it's just an early bloomer." She lifted her brows and shrugged.

A shadow passed across his features and he lifted his hand suddenly as if he'd just realized how intimate its location had been.

Growing impatient, Stampede shifted to the left. Jon reached forward to draw up the reins, his brows knitting together and the fine lines deepening. "Well, the sooner we get back to the house, the sooner I can get out with the truck to retrieve that ATV."

The moment of intimacy popped like a soap bubble, leaving Sylvie unsettled. Swallowing, she shifted in the saddle, desperate to find another comfortable position, something away from Jon's thighs and hips. Out of the corner of her eye, she spied a line of cows and their heifers moving toward the barn. Behind the predictable cattle lay the sweep of mountains. So much more beautiful than Bosnia's hills, with their battered houses and useless fields mined to the hilt.

Realizing he was headed home, Stampede picked up his pace and they rode the rest of the way in brisk silence.

When they reached the barn, Jon led the horse around to the well-beaten path to the house. He slid off Stampede's rump with ease. "Here you go." He held out his arms and guided her off. She didn't need the help but, still dealing with the emotions inside of her, she accepted it.

He shoved his Stetson down, hiding the frown she'd caught so briefly. "I'll see you at supper," he said.

The baby fluttered again and she put her hand on her tummy to try to soothe it. Or her. Or someone. "Thanks."

He led the horse to the barn, and she turned away just as he began to remove the tack.

What a strange afternoon, full of both discovery and fear. When the ATV had backfired, she'd hit the dirt like Nicholas Cage in one of his action films. She didn't even remember dropping the way she had. But she certainly remembered Jon's kisses afterward, swirling inside the pungent reminder of that horrible night.

She paused at the kitchen door. Then there was the radio. What *was* wrong with her? She'd absolutely hated that thing at the time. Stupid useless thing. But really, she shouldn't have totally destroyed it. She wasn't prone to fits of temper. She earned her rank and respect in the military with her calm, collected manner, not with outbursts like that.

She should never have taken the radio. She'd taped the mike key on Lawrence's radio so it would transmit continuously, and hidden it behind the back door. Then she'd taken Jon's and left.

Now, her action made no sense. She rigged the radios to act like a baby monitor, to ensure no one came into the house while she was out pushing the ATV to its rough-running limits. Pushing eastward as if to reach the rising sun, before it had yet to tint the sky.

Had she been running away from something? Or toward something she couldn't remember?

And when she'd realized her radio was no longer receiving, she'd lost her cool.

Alarm danced through her now, and she dared a peek

at Jon, way over by the barn. He remained busy with Stampede, his strong, muscular back to her as he swept the saddle off the horse. Stampede swung his head over and plowed into him, but Jon, so comfortable with horses, shoved him away. Her breath caught in her throat as she admired his powerful muscles. Did he use his strength in bed? Or did he keep it in close, well-controlled check?

What would it be like to be one of those women who'd known him intimately? They probably didn't mind bowing to his obvious strength and sexual prowess. He'd no doubt promise them full satisfaction.

Stop it, she ordered herself. These thoughts were just her body's self-preservation techniques so she didn't have to deal with the radio issue.

Besides, Jon was Rick's brother, and he was still grieving. The man who'd come for the truth would never make love to the kind of woman she really was.

Chapter 8

"Lawrence?"

At the sound of his name, the older man peered over the top of the book at Jon. Thankfully, this evening, Lawrence had chosen to read to himself the book on breastfeeding, and just a moment before, Jon had caught a glimpse of a graphic diagram he'd rather not hear described.

"Yep?" Lawrence asked.

Jon had forced himself to keep as busy as possible after he'd dropped Sylvie off, only because if he hadn't, he'd have immediately sought out Lawrence along the fence line, and the old man would have resented the work interruption.

Jon stole a glance at Purley and Michael, as they watched TV across the bunkhouse common room. "Can I talk to you? In private?"

Lawrence followed his gaze, his watery, pale eyes blinking over his reading glasses to the two men. When he focused on Jon again, he stood. Wordlessly he walked to the small bar refrigerator and pulled out two long-neck bottles of beer. Jon had seen them there through the glass door, and could have used them weeks ago, but they weren't offered.

"Let's step outside and check that pig. If Sylvie discovers he's escaped and scared the campers again, there'll be a few pork roasts in the freezer before Andrea returns."

They walked outside, and Jon let the screen door slam behind him. The warm night air carried the campers' voices and activities through the filter of the few trees. Jon cracked open his beer and followed Lawrence around the side of the house toward the zoo pens.

Jon's pace slowed. The kitchen light flooded the corner of the house. Sylvie had yet to go to bed.

What was she doing? Another bout of cleaning?

"You want to ask me something about her, or are you going to stare into the kitchen all night?" Lawrence's voice held a teasing note.

Jon resumed his walking, only realizing then that he'd come to a dead stop. "Sorry."

Lawrence took a long pull on his beer and when they reached the pen to find the darkened image of the pig rooting around, he set his beer bottle on the fence post.

"Nothing wrong with asking questions, son. So shoot."

A light from the front of the house cast long shadows around them. Ready to take the last swallow of cold beer, Jon froze. Had the light just come on? Had she heard them out here and was coming to investigate?

No. The light came from the ranch office, whose window glowed just beyond the end of the porch. The plain white sheers hung open and he spied Sylvie moving restlessly around.

"Does that a lot, lately, she does," Lawrence said. "I've seen her up well into the night. Ain't good for the baby."

"Often?" Jon wouldn't have noticed, as his tiny room faced the paddock. Lawrence's room faced the house.

"Too much restless energy, I guess," Lawrence said.

"Or too many bad dreams?"

Lawrence shot him a frown. Jon stared openly into the office window. Sylvie sat at her desk, her back to them. The lower half of the left window was raised, allowing for a breeze.

She stood up suddenly, threw back her short hair and stalked to the filing cabinet. Jon felt his eyes widen. Whoa. She wore nothing but a thin, flowing nightgown.

After grabbing some papers and a tissue from the neat stack of boxless tissues above it, she fell back down into her seat. Even with the loose, slinky nightgown on, he could see the rounded curves of her growing condition. She was all woman and growing more so each day.

For crying out loud, she should shut her curtains.

"You think she's having bad dreams?" Lawrence asked.

He pulled his attention away from her. "Yes. Why else would she be up?"

The older man shrugged. "Pregnancy changes a woman's sleeping habits."

"I've noticed that she has other unusual habits. Haven't you seen how she takes the tissues out of the box and discards the box?"

Lawrence didn't answer, so he persisted. "She's done that in her bedroom and in the office. See? On the filing cabinet?"

The old man squinted. "Yeah, I can see it."

"Aren't you going to ask why?"

"I already know. Sylvie told me she didn't like the picture on the carton."

"Then why buy the tissues? Most women buy tissue boxes not just for what's in them, but for how the carton will go with the decor."

"It was Andrea who bought them. She went to one of those warehouse stores and stocked up on tissues and toilet paper and gallons of pancake syrup."

"But Sylvie doesn't like the tissue boxes, so she removed the tissues, stacked them neatly and threw out the boxes."

Lawrence lifted his eyebrows. "Are you asking me or telling me?"

"I'm telling. And each of those boxes had a cute little teddy bear theme."

Lawrence nodded. "That would be Andrea. She must have thought they were cute."

"Each of those boxes had a picture of a teddy bear doing something. The one in her room was driving an army truck."

"Oh."

Jon checked his rising agitation. "She's had a lot of free time to remove the tissues and stack them in neat piles."

"You think she's doing that at night? So she's having trouble sleeping. She's running a ranch, a campground, and is pregnant and unmarried. She's got a lot on her mind."

"There's more. Do you remember when I asked you about the radio that went missing?"

Lawrence nodded again. A passing moth danced around him, but he waved it away.

"I found it later. It had been smashed and ground into the dirt road beside the campground office."

"Who do you think did it?"

"Sylvie. She ran over it with the ATV."

Lawrence's eyes widened. "Sylvie? How do you know that?"

"I found small hunks of it imbedded in the tread of the ATV's tire after you left the line shack." No need to go into detail about how he happened to notice the tires in the first place. "When I asked her about it, she tried to run away."

"Sylvie? She's never run away from anything."

"After the ATV died, it backfired. A second later she had me pinned on the ground, while she scanned the area. I've scared her before, too, Lawrence. She's edgy. And you did say she's changed."

Lawrence grabbed his beer again and took a gulp, before realizing it was nearly empty. He glared at it. "Well, that's true. She's not the same. I'd just chalked it up to her pregnancy and retirement." He studied Jon in the dim light. "What do you think it is?"

"It's post-traumatic stress disorder. I've seen it in police officers, but it's not reserved for cops and soldiers. We've had suspects who suffered from it, as well."

Lawrence hooked the beer bottle between his index and middle finger and swung it pensively at his thigh. Finally he nodded. "I've heard of it. In fact, I had a cousin who had it. Got it from the war. They called it shell shock back then."

He tapped the bottle on his thigh. "I can't say I have much experience with it. Sylvie's grandfather, Stanley Mitchell, tried to enlist with me in '39. I was underage. We were ranchers and Stan had just acquired this place. When he found out he'd been turned down because he was a rancher, he told the recruiters how old I really was, and that he needed me to work the land, as well. Oh, I saw red that day. Damn fool Mitchell couldn't go to war, so he made sure I couldn't, either.'' He shook his head. ''Ironic, if what you say is true, sixty-some years later, the granddaughter ends up with the post-war stress.''

''It adds up, Lawrence. Sensitive nerves, sleeplessness, fits of anger. I just can't figure out...''

''What to do?''

Jon shook his head. ''No. There are viable treatments for it. I'm sure some of them will have to wait until the baby's born, but she should see her doctor for it right away. She might not even know—''

''Nor will she say anything, son. She's like her grandfather. Stubborn as this pot-bellied pig when he's hungry.''

She was that, all right. ''I wondered why she took out her frustrations on the radio. Sure it acted up occasionally, but she was pretty brutal with it. There's not a piece left that's bigger than my thumbnail. And if she's going to—''

He didn't want to finish his sentence, so Lawrence did it for him. ''Get mad, she might take out her anger on her child? Your nephew or niece?''

Jon threw him a sharp look. ''What has Sylvie told you?''

''Nothing. She tells me zilch. But I haven't lived nearly eighty years for nothing. Listen to me, Jon, my boy. She wouldn't hurt her baby. She's determined to have this child, come hell or high water.''

''Then why was she so brutal to the radio?''

''Figure out what the radio means to her and you've got your reason why she smashed it.'' Lawrence patted Jon's back encouragingly. ''I'm supposed to go into town

with her tomorrow. Just for some groceries and look into
those come-alongs. Why don't you go instead? Take her
out to supper. We'll hold down the fort and it'll give you
a chance to talk to her. Maybe you can get her to tell her
doctor about her symptoms.''

Jon couldn't imagine Sylvie meekly obeying him, but
he doubted she'd listen to anyone else, either, even Lawrence. He nodded slowly. Perhaps a bit of time away
from the ranch might get her to open up about Rick.

Damn. He'd told himself to bide his time. Let her start
that conversation. He wouldn't force her.

Not like he'd forced the two of them around, while
helping himself to the sweet skin of her neck and shoulders.

Lawrence gave him one last pat and sauntered back
toward the bunkhouse. Jon glanced over at the office window, finding Sylvie still at her desk, her shoulders
hunched a bit too tightly. She needed him to push her
into getting help, whether she admitted it or not.

And with his steamroller style, he could do it.

Jon didn't bother to knock at the door. If she could
display herself in just her nightgown to the whole front
yard, she wouldn't mind him walking in on her.

She looked up when the door swung open. Fatigue
hung from her expression, and yet the shoulders straightened sharply when she saw who entered.

''Working late?'' he asked, keeping his voice bland.

''Just finishing up some bill paying. I'm going to bed
shortly.'' Her mouth pursed to a firm slash across her
face.

Had he not seen her through the window, he would
have believed her. She stood up briskly, and aligned her
invoices into a businesslike stack before returning them

to the filing cabinet, a ridiculous action considering her attire. And her damn shaking hands. He could see how Lawrence, way out in the front yard, hadn't believed there was a problem. She hid it well.

"Is there something you need?" she asked him. Even her voice sounded brisk and professional. Yeah, of course she was, dressed in a silk nightgown meant more for the privacy of a bedroom. One that had a wide, king-size bed. And decent curtains to shut out the world.

"I just stopped by to tell you that I'll be taking you into town tomorrow."

"Lawrence is, thanks."

He ignored the dismissal. "No. I am. We switched duties. We need to talk."

She slammed the filing cabinet closed. "We've already been through this, Jon—"

"It's not about Rick. It's about you."

"Me?" She gaped at him. Well, finally he'd caught her off guard.

"Why don't we have a bite to eat while we're in town? We can go to some old place you haven't been for a while."

"What's all this about?" Her expression hardened, her eyes narrowing. "I don't want a date, Jon, thank you all the same."

"You need to see your doctor for more than just the baby, Sylvie. You haven't been sleeping or eating right."

"I'm fine."

He gritted his teeth. The Mitchell stubbornness. Well, he couldn't say he hadn't been warned about it. His voice low and soft, he called upon all the patience he'd acquired as a police officer. "I'm only thinking of what's best for you, Sylvie."

She stopped fussing with some files on top of the cabinet. Immediately, she brushed back a loose line of blond hair. He spotted her lips parting.

Had he said her name any differently? She seemed to soften when it had slid from his mouth.

And when she glanced at him, her eyes, no longer the cold gemstones they'd been a moment before, melted into a fluid, translucent blue green. The color of a deep, dark ravine filled with rushing water, freshly melted from some mountain snowpack.

She took a step toward him, and her nightgown danced around her body. He tore his gaze from the swells and dips of the silky material and found, to his amazement, desperation in her eyes.

Desperation? He couldn't move.

"Is that what you really want, Jon? To talk at the local diner about my sleeping habits? Or are you here to finish off what you started out by the line shack?"

Gone was the tight mouth, the ramrod-straight posture and the hard look. They'd dissolved like the sugar in his hot morning coffee, leaving him both cautious and curious as he watched a soft pout form on her parted lips. Her shoulders dipped as she reached for the low collar of her nightgown.

Her hands still shook, though.

Slowly she slipped each tiny button free, and then, in one languid movement, she shrugged her shoulders. Her delicate nightgown slid like warm water to the floor.

Chapter 9

Jon swallowed, unable to move. She wore only the slimmest of panties, a plain white pair cut high and sweeping low below her slightly burgeoning belly.

She was ripening fast before his eyes. The mere glimpses he'd had earlier today didn't do her body justice. Her heavy breasts rose and fell rhythmically, and below them was the same softly rounded belly he'd cupped today. The one that cradled his brother's child.

He shook off the dangerous desire and stormed past her to the windows. Yanking shut the thin curtains, he growled, "If you don't mind, I think this sort of thing doesn't need to be exhibited to all the world."

He spun back around in time to catch her slight frown and lush lips biting together. She bent down and pulled the voluminous nightgown up past her knees, her hips, her full, lavish breasts. "I guess you've answered my question."

He'd expected her tone to be petulant, but it was hurt that rang clearly through the room. He cringed inwardly.

"Sylvie," he said, coming up in front of her and gently doing up the tiny buttons, his uncooperative hands fumbling with the silk, as if they didn't want any part of his sudden prudish behavior. His hands had no idea how little self-control he had. Or perhaps they did. "Would you have done this kind of thing a year ago?"

Her eyebrows flew up in shock. "What do you mean?"

"I'm betting you wouldn't have. But look at you, Sylvie. You can't sleep. You can't eat. And you have nightmares, don't you?"

Surprise struck filled her features. "How did you know?"

His hands settled on her shoulders and he revisited the urge to pull her close. "What happened to you in Bosnia was traumatic. You lost someone you cared about. You watched him die—"

She pushed him back. Spinning around, she finished the task he'd abandoned. Jon could see her hands shaking as his had. "I can't talk about it. So please don't say any more."

He caught her and turned her, firming up his grip on her shoulders so she couldn't escape. "I'm not forcing you to tell me anything, Sylvie!" Immediately he calmed and, seeing she'd shut her eyes, he ordered, "Sylvie? Sylvie, open your eyes!"

When she obeyed him, he went on. "Listen, I don't want you to relive that night over and over again. Don't tell me anything, if you don't want to. But listen! You're suffering from emotional shock. Maybe post-traumatic stress disorder. You went from a traumatic situation straight into a totally different life-style, without any transition. And pregnant at the same time. Life has just beat up on you, and you have to tell your doctor about it. Understand?''

She didn't move or speak or even blink. In him rose an indignant fury at the military, who would counsel soldiers returning from dangerous theaters of operation like Afghanistan but who'd allowed Sylvie to slip through their system's cracks. ''You have to tell your doctor. Understand?'' he repeated.

He watched as the hollow pain blurred her eyes. She remained rigid, staring at him with hurt and quiet begging until the truth slammed hard into him.

He could never again ask her about Rick. Never.

He bit back the full extent of his decision. In two months the summer would be over and he'd return to Toronto. To the job he loved and at which he'd been determined to excel, to fight back against the crime that had killed his father.

To his lonely little house in a small town outside of the city.

The house filled with Rick's untouched effects.

Despite the military's promises of a full report, he knew he'd never learn what really happened. He couldn't fight back against the crime that had killed his brother. And it would be wrong to force the truth from Sylvie.

Wrong? He gave himself a mental smack. It was more than wrong. It would devastate her, and who knew how the pain would affect her baby, his brother's child?

The futility drifted between them like a cold draft, and he dragged her close to him to squeeze it away. Even as he clung to her, an overwhelming part of him ignored his fragmented good sense. Hormones surged into action, sloshing around inside him like scalding coffee in a paper cup during a high-speed car chase.

He should leave now. What good would it do either of them if he stuck around? She needed a doctor, not a cop with the courage to battle street crime in their country's biggest city but not enough guts to open his dead brother's barrack box.

And he didn't need to torture himself with Sylvie, who exuded a ripening lust he should *in no way* sample. He'd discounted sibling rivalry weeks ago, but, hey, maybe sibling rivalry was the root of this insane attraction. After all, Rick, as young as he was, had caught her eye.

Jon bristled. He'd never wanted for women, even when some roving female eye had seen his wedding band. During his marriage, he hadn't fooled around, but the women had still offered. Sylvie, however, had been nothing but cool to him. Until out by the line shack. And here, tonight. Had he wanted her only because she hadn't offered herself? And when she had, did the allure lose its appeal?

Maybe there was something about wanting what didn't belong to him and never could. Something that made him ache with need.

Sylvie wasn't his. Period. And he'd better get used to it.

So why couldn't he let go of her?

"I'm taking you in to see your doctor, Sylvie. Tomorrow."

Snuggled against his shirt, inhaling the scent of Jon's fresh shower and hot skin, she nodded. "All right."

She found it easier to stay buried in his arms than to face him. The torrent of desperation that had hit her a few minutes ago slowly drained to a narrow trickle. Since leaving Bosnia, she'd waited for emotion, any emotion to fill her again, but there had been nothing. One pale day after another. Then Jon's kisses this afternoon had unlocked a door inside of her, and instead of all the welcoming life returning, only desperation flooded in.

All she'd wanted was to feel. Something, anything, and with Jon here, she'd wanted to feel so badly, she'd peeled away her nightgown to seek fulfillment on an instinctive, animal level. Pure, raw sex she'd heard so much about but never experienced.

Abruptly Jon pulled back, and cool air flowed in between them. Breaking the embrace completely, she walked over and lifted a tissue from the neat pile on the filing cabinet. She dabbed her eyes. Then, finding the action too frivolous, she gave them both a harsh swipe. "You're right, you know."

"About what?"

"I would never have behaved like this a year ago. I knew something was wrong. First I chalked it up to hormones, then to just making the transition to civilian life." She drew in her breath and, feeling a bit restored, she straightened. "Today, as I watched you lead Stampede back to the paddock, I knew something had to be wrong with me. And just now…"

She couldn't mention her outrageous behavior of a moment ago. And the look on his pity-filled face was answer enough to the question she'd silently posed to him. Whatever scrap of lust he'd had back there at the line shack had dissipated. Especially now he'd seen her ugly, distorted body, all swollen and due to swell more. She must look awful in the harsh fluorescent light, breasts huge and belly threatening to hide her feet from her view.

He was only interested in the health of his nephew or niece. That much was clear. There could never be anything more between them.

* * *

"Well," she said, slipping into the most private booth in the town's best—and only—diner. "The doctor said he couldn't give me anything like a prescription for antidepressants, but he had some pamphlets and suggested I take a few natural remedies." She pulled out a prescription paper. "Evening primrose oil and some extra vitamins."

"Sounds good."

She smiled at Jon as he waited for her to continue. "More importantly, he did agree that it was post-traumatic stress disorder. He says I have *all* the classic symptoms." She gave a shaky laugh, trying to sound upbeat. "You know, funny thing is, I feel better. Haven't taken anything for it, yet, but I feel so…relieved."

He returned her smile. He'd been quiet all morning, but she chalked it up to the tension of her going to the doctor. And of him dealing with her behavior last night when a crazy part of her had begged for him to…to show her how to feel again.

Or was he just plain embarrassed because she'd stripped down naked in front of him? Would their relationship ever get past "uncomfortable"?

She cringed inwardly.

When the waitress came, they ordered a couple of sandwiches, Jon's with a beer and hers with a large milk. Even food seemed to have more appeal all of a sudden. She actually looked forward to it.

"One thing the doctor had said I should do more often is smile. Seems studies have revealed that it helps to release some chemicals in the brain. And if we don't feel like smiling, we should anyway. And avoid depressing people, too."

Jon gave her a wry grin. "Stay away from Lawrence, then. Last night, after I left you, I had to listen to another hour of the dangers of postpartum depression.'' He rolled his eyes and shook his head. "Makes me long for the days when all we talked about were itchy bellies and stretch marks.''

She burst out laughing. Lord, it felt so good. "I should have joined in on that conversation, being the only one on the ranch with actual experience with stretch marks. Even Andrea hasn't had them.''

They fell silent and after a moment he asked, "When do you expect your father to return?''

"Two more weeks, but they're going back out again. He called after you left last night.'' Even now his call confused her. Dad hadn't been there for her for so long. Yet, she couldn't define how she felt about it now he seemed to be reaching out to her.

"What did he want?''

"I don't really know.'' She peered at Jon as the waitress delivered the drinks. "I think he just wanted to talk. So we talked about the line shack and such. Then he asked me how the doctor appointments were, if I took vitamins, and made sure I hadn't been riding.'' She paused. "Do you think Andrea prompted him?''

"I've never met her, so how would I know?''

She pursed her lips. "Perhaps she did, but there was something in his voice. Like he used to talk to me before my mother died.'' She pushed away the dismal images with a bright smile. *Positive thoughts. Positive thoughts.*

She took a sip from her milk. "Thank you, Jon.''

He tipped his beer to her, his handsome face slightly cocky. "Anytime.''

Deciding she liked the way he lifted his right eyebrow, she leaned forward and looked hard at his beautiful, relaxed features. But she couldn't fathom what he might be thinking and for that moment she didn't care. "I know we're supposed to go check out the come-alongs and the jacks we'll have to rent, but I want to go somewhere else. Someplace that's special to me. Want to see it?''

A light flashed in his eyes. "Sure." When his smile returned, the slow easy movement of his lips stirred warmth deep within her.

Lust. Sex. Something left over from last night. A part of her that still hadn't realized that Jon would never fill the void inside of her. Not when he'd soon return to his police officer life in Ontario.

Of course, if anything—she held her breath a moment—were to come of the time they spend together…well, she wouldn't stop it.

Chapter 10

The ridge stood higher than she remembered, but then again, back in her youth she hadn't been carrying anything more than a light backpack with a can of soda pop and a chocolate bar. Now she carried twenty more pounds of fat and baby. She allowed Jon to pull her up the last five feet.

"This used to be my favorite place in the whole world," she said between pants. "But after today I have serious doubts."

Jon smiled as he scanned the wide eastern horizon. "I wish I'd had a place like this when I was growing up. Look at the view!"

Their outing had taken a heart-straining hour, but Jon was right. This ridge was special. The air, freshened by the evergreens and glaciers on its trip down the mountains, had a tang of its own. Sylvie stood straight and tall, drawing in the wonderful scent. In front of her the stretch of prairie shimmered in green and gold strips below the vast, clear sky.

Squinting down to her right, she spied the town of Trail. She turned her head slightly, and found the line shack. Beyond, the tiny buildings of the ranch looked like angular dashes of white. "Can you find the ranch?"

Jon shielded his eyes. "There. We took that back road. I dare say you've skirted the ranch on more than one occasion in your youth."

She laughed. "Feels deliciously wicked playing hookey, doesn't it? Once when I was thirteen, three of us girls skipped school. We'd forged notes from our parents to let us off for the day." She stopped a moment, savoring a small smile as it lingered after her words. "Me, Lucy and Denise. We'd been friends all our lives. All thirteen years. And we'd decided that day to form a special club."

The smile drifted away. "We'd thought we were the most unfortunate kids in the whole province. Maybe we were. I'd lost my mother. Lucy's father had been killed in some robbery at his garage and her best friend before me had died in this nasty car accident that killed the whole family the same day as her father had died. And Denise, well, she was always the loneliest. She always wanted children and the happily-ever-after stuff. She hasn't found it yet. I should call her."

Jon watched her. She could feel his gaze linger on her skin. "They're still here?"

"Yes. You know, that day we blazed a trail up to this very spot. Actually, I think the trail was already here, but we were convinced we'd done all the work."

"How did you get to the start of the trail?"

"Funny you should ask." She flicked up her eyebrows. "We borrowed Denise's father's pickup. He was in farming once, but he got out of it later and became an accountant. Lucy, being the daughter of Trail's only tow truck operator, drove. I was going to drive back. I was so excited. All I'd driven were tractors.''

"What happened?"

"Well, it didn't quite turn out as well as you think. Lucy got the truck stuck. So, we figured we'd let it sit while we hiked up here." She laughed. "I don't remember our logic for leaving it, but it sounded really good back then."

"Teenagers are rarely logical."

"How true. Anyway, when the three of us got up here that day, we sat facing each other and made a pact."

Jon threw her an amused look. "I can't wait to hear this."

"We vowed to be happy. We promised each other we'd do anything to be happy. Of course, Denise, the prissiest of us, wanted clarification on what we meant by 'do anything.' Lucy told her flat-out we deserved happiness after all we'd endured, and just shut up and agree."

"Endured?"

Sylvie smiled. "I know. Compare my life now with back then, and my teenage years look like a Sunday picnic. After that, we climbed back down."

John smiled. "To the stuck truck? How'd you get it free? Steal Lucy's father's tow truck?"

Sylvie feigned a guilty look. "Not quite. While we were gone, Lawrence found it and called the police, figuring something awful had happened to Denise's father. The police then called her house and got her mother all freaked out. After a while, of course, we arrived back at the scene of the crime, only to find the police and a bunch of local men, mostly fathers of our school friends, ready to start searching the woods for Denise's dad.''

''Where was he?''

''He was still out plowing his fields. Didn't know a thing was wrong. You know, I never did get to drive the truck. Dad grounded me for a month. He used to be really strict.''

A curious sense of belonging rippled through her. Who would figure she'd feel such emotion while recalling her father's punishment?

''Must have been why you joined the military. To drive enough trucks to catch up with Lucy and Denise.''

She shook her head and turned to watch the vista. ''No. I enlisted to escape the ranch. It wasn't doing well back then, like most of the ranches during the late eighties. I used to think back then that Dad should have just dissolved the whole operation and moved into a retirement apartment.'' She sighed, her foolish reminiscing watering her eyes. ''Dad wasn't that old, yet I figured he was ancient.''

She sagged against one of the large outcroppings of rock. ''I'm sorry. I'm starting to sound maudlin. It's been such a good day. I don't want to ruin it.''

He grunted out a strangled word, something she didn't catch. After two long strides, he reached her and, automatically, she fell into his open arms. How good it felt.

He spoke into her hair. ''Don't expect to be able to turn off the waterworks right away. Give it some time.''

''But I feel so much better. I mean, when the doctor and I talked, we went through the whole list of symptoms and…well, it's just…it was so clear what was wrong. The constant worry, reliving all that had happened.''

Jon stiffened in her arms and she shut her eyes, knowing he expected more.

She clenched her jaw. *Oh, please don't ask. Not now. Not ever.*

She felt him tighten his grip on her. *Oh, don't let me go. Forget I spoke.*

The minutes lingered and Sylvie gave herself up to the embrace.

Too soon Jon released her. She straightened her clothing. "Let's forget the last few minutes, okay? You must think I'm a real flake."

Surprise flared in his eyes. "A flake? Why would you think that?"

"All right, maybe not a flake, but a fool." Her mind raced for some way to change the subject. Anything to lead the conversation away from what had happened.

Too late. Like a movie in front of her eyes, she relived it all. Rick, wounded, in the back of the truck. She, on top of him, crazy with fear that she'd die a virgin—without ever experiencing the joy of lovemaking—

A knot of shame choked her. One night of total idiocy left her private dead and her pregnant.

She wiped her face with cold hands. "I should have realized what was happening to me weeks ago. It's not like post-traumatic stress has never been discussed in the military. PTSD had been part of the briefings we had to attend before going to Bosnia. It's just that my own debriefings afterward were practically nonexistent because I came back earlier than the rest of the company. I kept thinking my symptoms were just hormones. I'm such a fool."

"No." He shook his head, almost violently, still keeping his distance. "You're neither. In fact, I have to say, I've never met a woman with your strength and smarts."

She bumped into the outcropping when she backed away from him. "Me?"

"Sure? Who would have suggested straightening that old line shack instead of tearing it down?"

"It hasn't been done successfully yet."

"It doesn't matter if it's ever successful. The idea is good enough to try. Lawrence, with all his vast experience, didn't consider it. But you used your experience and resourcefulness to try a different approach. Like they say, you thought outside the box."

She stared at him. Was something good coming from her tour of Bosnia? Something besides the baby growing inside of her?

Pride swelled in her at the sight of Jon's admiring smile and the sound of his encouraging voice. Incredible. Twice in one day she'd felt a kind of hope, anticipation that even the tiny baby within had not yet produced.

Jon turned back to the vista they'd come to see. He was talking on about how great the scene looked, but she couldn't focus on his words. Instead she leaned against the rock and watched him, hoping the weeks left would go so much slower than what was already behind her.

Because she wanted Jon to be a friend and more. He glanced over his shoulder at her, a look that was both warm and haunted.

But friends don't lie to each other, a demon inside of her taunted. *And neither do lovers.*

The knot returned to her throat. Maybe she should tell him the truth about Rick's death and risk the court martial. His need for the truth lingered under the surface all the time. And as much as he didn't show it, he still begrudged her keeping it to herself.

She could easily take the heat off her, but she'd have to omit the selfish part where she hadn't wanted to die a virgin...and omit most of what Rick had said.

An omission was as bad as a lie.

But Jon deserved to know Rick's last hours. It was worth a court martial. She reached out her hand.

A pain struck hard at her abdomen, punching out her breath and weakening her knees.

"Oh!" She collapsed onto the rock floor, just as another agonizing jab clawed her again. Through a blur of tears, she caught Jon spinning around, and after one swift stride, reaching for her. One of her hands met his arm, the other cradled her belly.

"What is it?" His rushed voice pierced her pain.

"I...I don't know. I stood up straight and this sharp pain just hit me." She blinked his worried features back into focus. Her heart throbbed in her throat, choking her. "Oh, God, Jon, I hope it's not the baby!"

The millisecond that the doctor left the examination room, Jon plowed over to him. "How is she?"

The doctor stepped back, startled. "Would you like to go in, Mr. Cahill? Sylvie said she'd like to see you."

His heart racing, Jon charged into the room. The same one he'd taken Sylvie to that first day they'd met. His heart had been in his throat all that day, but this time...hell, it seemed lodged there worse than ever.

Sylvie lay on her side, an ice pack on her swollen abdomen. Jon threw her a questioning look. Then one to the doctor who'd followed him back in.

"She's pulled a muscle." The doctor peered disapprovingly over his glasses at her. Sylvie looked away. "She shouldn't have taken up mountain climbing halfway through her pregnancy."

"The trail was a bit steep in parts. It wasn't mountain climbing," Sylvie mumbled.

"Your abdominal muscles are stretched enough, and

during pregnancy, ligaments loosen. No more long walks. And no walking at all for the next few days, either.''

Jon tunneled shaking fingers through his hair, afraid to feel relief yet. ''The baby?''

The doctor faced him, his face still bland. ''Is fine. In fact, he's quite active for being so young. She's only strained a couple of lower, supporting muscles and a groin muscle, though I suspect that one not as much. Have her keep some ice on it for the next few hours, then she can alternate between warm packs and cold packs. Bring her back in if she doesn't improve in a day or two.''

''Thank you.'' His heart still pounding, Jon closed the door behind the doctor. Damn it, Sylvie should have known better.

Yeah, and he should have known better, too. She'd smiled and chatted all the way up the steep climb and he hadn't suspected she might not be able to manage the hike. They'd both still been reeling with the almost-euphoria of knowing the cause of her erratic behavior. He'd been giddy with relief as they ate lunch, then she'd suggested a bit of hookey from the ranch.

He should have been paying more attention to her needs.

Well, from now on he would. ''Feeling up to going home?''

She shoved away the cold pack and struggled to the sitting position. ''Are you going to treat me like an invalid if I say 'yes, let's go home'?''

He offered his hand, but she brushed it away. Anger rose in him. She had no plans to take it easy. ''Sylvie, you *are* going to take it easy.''

''I'm fine.''

''The hell you are. If you don't do as the doctor says,

I'm moving into your house and camping out in front of your bedroom door.''

She opened her mouth, no doubt to protest, but said nothing. A blush feathered its way up her neck as she pulled down on her shirt. By the time she allowed him to help her off the table, her face glowed bright pink. "All right. You win."

"Now you're talking." He liked winning. And this easy little victory felt damn good because Sylvie didn't give him many. And yeah, he also liked the idea of paying attention to her needs. All of her needs.

A familiar need of his own heated his groin, and to cover the unbidden lust he straightened the paper sheet she'd been lying on.

Forget it, Cahill. She's off-limits. He should focus on being grateful that she and the baby were okay. She had nothing more than a pulled muscle that was already straining to accommodate her swelling womb.

The one filled with his only relative. The one that had been pressed against his palm out on the range, and the one whose skin, smooth and pale he'd seen last night. So begging to be kissed.

He gritted his teeth. "Let's go. And remember, Sylvie, you stay in your bedroom and don't do a thing. Or else I'm moving into your hallway."

Sylvie had relented and retired to her room, not before dropping a few of the PTSD pamphlets the doctor had given her on the kitchen table. Jon had seen the stack during supper and knew there were several more, probably in her room, waiting to be read. He'd only come in for some ice cubes, choosing the errand over Lawrence's latest lesson of the actual mechanics of a vaginal delivery.

Jon was probably the only officer on the entire police force in Toronto who'd never had the privilege of delivering a baby, something of which he was rather secretly proud. There had always been a hospital or an ambulance close enough to save him the terror. Besides, Michael and Purley were more likely than him to need the information that Lawrence was reciting. He wouldn't be around for Sylvie's delivery.

Popping the ice out of the tray into a small container, Jon pushed aside the disappointment the idea of leaving created. He'd be here only for another month. Get Sylvie back on the road to recovery, somehow take Allister aside when he got back next week and explain to him what she'd gone through, maybe suggest the older man read those pamphlets.

Jon set the container on the counter while he filled the ice cube tray with tap water. An unbidden thought struck him like a sucker punch. He'd never feel Sylvie under him. Even now the taste of her skin from out by the line shack and the vision she'd created in her office simmered his blood.

She wasn't his. No more than his ex-wife had been his when she finally admitted she was pregnant with another man's child. A thick sigh seethed through his gritted teeth. How the hell did he get mixed up with another pregnant woman? A woman who wasn't carrying just a baby, but a secret she refused to reveal.

God forgive him, he'd give his eyeteeth to spend one night in her bed, secret be damned.

All right, he'd admitted the dangerous notion. Now forget it. Looking to distract himself, he grabbed one of Sylvie's pamphlets and hastily scanned it.

It listed some classic symptoms, dry statistics and a

few addresses at which more information could be obtained. Then the pamphlet underneath caught his eye. "Spousal information on PTSD: don't let it destroy your relationship."

Still holding the ice bucket, he flipped open the narrow paper.

Sharing a traumatic experience can draw people closer, and the resulting emotions can manifest as romantic feelings. When the sharing is done with a spouse or partner, PTSD, properly treated, can help to strengthen a relationship, but sometimes a third party may be involved. It is necessary to understand that the romantic feelings may simply be a manifestation of the shared stress or grief or whatever initially triggered the PTSD.

Jon dropped the pamphlet like a hot potato. Damn, that was what had happened to him and Sylvie!

He'd been grieving, too. At first Sylvie had been a place where he could assign his grief and anger, but later, as the weeks rolled by and his anger eased, a different emotion arose.

Those warm, fuzzy feelings, those hot flashes of lust where he wanted nothing more than to carry Sylvie to her bed and explore her ripening body, they were all his body's way of trying to find someone to grieve with. After all, he had no one. Rick had been his only relative and, unable to bear the thought of losing him, Jon had looked to share his grief.

The hard, desperate lump inside of him burned his gut, leaving him with one brutal solution.

Until he left, he must not let the grief and stress trick

him into thinking he and Sylvie should be anything more than friends. They had to focus on her health and nothing else.

Sylvie smiled at him over breakfast the next day. "Since we didn't get into the rental store yesterday, would you like to go in with me this morning?"

Purley and Michael had eaten early and left. Michael's shoulder was bothering him today, an injury from a cattle drive years ago, and he needed Purley's help in the barn. Lawrence, however, lingered over his second cup of coffee.

Jon glanced at him. "Don't you think Lawrence would be a better choice?"

"Don't look at me." Lawrence didn't lift his head from yet another library book, *The First Year of Life*. This book was infinitely preferable to the previous ones, but Jon wished Lawrence would restrict his reading to the evening. "Got the vet coming this afternoon. One of the cows needs looking at."

Sylvie frowned. "Nothing serious, I hope."

"Don't think so." He shut his book. "She's just not feeding her young 'un, that's all. You two go on ahead and get that equipment. We'll be ready for you."

Jon's heart stalled in his chest. Did Sylvie have to look at him as though she wanted him to pull her into one of his stupid embraces and hold her until he gave in to the inappropriate lust and dragged her off to bed? She had no idea how long the list of reasons against this relationship was becoming.

But, hell, he'd told her he'd help her and that meant with the line shack, too. He swallowed. "I'll be ready whenever you are."

* * *

"And he needs a new heart," Sylvie explained as they pulled into the rental store's parking lot. She wasn't used to asking men out on a date. Had she rushed her words of explanation?

Jon parked the truck in the first available spot before looking at her thoroughly confused. "Who needs a new heart?"

She gaped at him. "Haven't you been listening?"

He looked as if he'd been a million miles away, his expression not just distant but also deeply sad. Was the ranch boring him? Was he thinking of his life back home? Was the fact that she carried his nephew or niece now losing its appeal?

Or was he thinking that since she would probably never reveal the last hours of his brother's life, it was time to throw in the towel and leave?

She could tell him the barest facts, the ones Tirouski had insisted she keep to herself, but that would precipitate a stream of events worse than anything she'd witnessed in the military. And Jon would eventually learn the whole truth.

He shoved the shift lever into park. "All right. Let's start at the beginning. Who needs a heart?"

"Fred Barker," she started again with a long exhalation, "he's one of the hands over at the Cavanaugh ranch. He's had congenital heart failure for a few years and has been on a donor list for nearly as long. Well, they've found a heart for him. He's headed for Calgary's Heart Center as we speak, but he won't be able to afford the antirejection drugs. They cost thousands a month."

Jon let out a whistle. "Insurance?"

"Well, the medicare doesn't cover that cost, nor do most of the major insurance companies, but there is one that will cover a percentage. The rancher's wife got it for her workers at the first sign of trouble, thankfully, but the share he'll have to pay is still substantial and he'll have to take the drugs for the rest of his life. That's why they're having this fund-raiser.''

''A dinner?''

''Dinner, dance, auction and *silent* auction.'' She licked her lips, hating how they seemed to dry up so suddenly. Jon's gaze flickered down at her tongue and a hot tendril of nervous tension twisted around her spine.

''I want to go,'' she went on. ''I know we probably won't find any bargains there, but it's for a good cause and I know the man quite well. Plus, a silent auction is always fun. Trying to outbid your neighbor, sneaking over to Marg's brownies to write your name down and outbid the others without anyone catching you. You've tasted her brownies.'' They'd had them yesterday, and Michael had stolen the last two on his way out after supper.

He nodded. ''I can well imagine that the bidding would be fast and furious for a tray of them. But as for the dance—''

''I promise I won't dance. If you come, you'll be able to make sure of that,'' she hedged. ''Anyway, I'd like to take you to thank you for all your help this summer.'' There. She'd said it. Now for his answer....

''You don't need to thank me.''

She bit her lower lip, resisting the urge to lick it again and reveal how nervous she felt. Jon, however, didn't miss it. Only when his stare drifted down again did she realize that there was more to it than his simple observation.

He looked like a child with no money in a candy store.

She strengthened her voice. ''Marg says that the big items donated are going to be auctioned off during the dance. She says there are a few baby items, too. Maybe we can stay for them.'' *Please say yes.*

She hated the thought of begging, even the silent kind. But the candy-store look had hardened, causing her heart to sink like a stone in a pond.

With fear crawling up her spine, she waited for Jon to stop studying the damn steering wheel and look at her.

Fear. She shut her eyes, willing back the most fearful memory she had.

…scrambling under her truck, dodging the screams of deadly bullets while she yelled at Rick, asking him if he'd been shot…believing him when he said he hadn't been….

Stop it! Asking Jon on a date wasn't as fearful. But what if he said no? She was carrying his brother's baby. Would he think it was wrong to date her? To see her as a sexual being?

Hadn't he already considered her so? With his kisses out by the line shack? And yet she knew he regretted every single burning kiss he'd pressed on her.

She braced herself when his lips thinned and pursed.

Jon tilted his head. He needed a moment to pull his mind out of the gutter and focus on her words. He shouldn't be thinking of her tongue wasting its worth by licking her lips, when it could be in his mouth, driving him to distraction. ''When did you hear about this auction?''

''Everyone's known about Fred's need for years.'' She sounded nervous. ''But one of the women who runs the community center called this morning with the news and asked us if we could donate something for the dinner or the auction.''

He narrowed his eyes. Benefit auction donations could

range from something as benign as a rusting baler suitable only as a lawn ornament, all the way up to the terrifying eligible-bachelor-for-the-evening donation. He'd nearly got roped into one of them before. "What did you have in mind?"

"A ham and my mother's scalloped potato recipe." She shot him a suspicious look. "What did you think?"

Relief rushed through him. He shrugged. "Nothing."

She bit her lip, and her hand dropped to her belly. When his gaze followed, she hastily found the fresh vent levers to adjust instead. "What I've been trying to ask is, would you take me to the benefit dinner? And sit with me at the auction? I haven't been to one in years, and, call me unsophisticated, but I find them very exciting."

He should have seen this suggestion coming a mile away, but somehow it escaped him. Dinner? And an auction? Waiting this morning for her, he'd sternly told himself to cool things between them. He'd be going home soon. Sure he wanted to be part of the baby's life, and he'd meant it when he'd said he would be, but hell, the relationship between him and Sylvie had to cool.

When he didn't answer, Sylvie threw open the truck door and climbed out, muttering something about there'd better be a washroom in the rental store.

He stared at her. What the hell was he doing? Turning down a charity auction and dinner? He grimaced. Timidity wasn't part of his makeup. He could balance the growing attraction that seemed based only on shared grief with a simple charity dinner. He was a police officer, for crying out loud. Each day in Toronto, he weighed the risks of his job against public safety all the time. Above all that, he was an adult. He could temper his own inappropriate responses.

"Sylvie!"

She stopped by the front door and waited for him to trot up to her before she spoke. "All right, so Trail's hardly a mecca for social functions, and short of asking you to see the latest preteen movie now playing, there isn't much we can do here."

Her swallow didn't go unnoticed. She was nervous and he was just adding to it with his ambivalence. But he had something more important to say first.

"Lawrence said something to me yesterday about Veterans Affairs."

Her eyes stayed cool, the emeralds returning with chilliness. "Yes, Lawrence should be drawing his pension, now, but he says as long as he—"

He interrupted her. "What I mean to say is that Veterans Affairs can help *you*. You've received an injury, per se, as a direct result of a tour of duty. I remember reading in the papers how because all the World War II vets are dying, they have the monies and manpower to help the soldiers of today."

"Jon—"

"No, Sylvie, your doctor has already diagnosed you and has told you this is a physiological condition. You can't take the medication needed, but you can see if you're entitled to other—" he searched for the proper words to use "—compensation? You're suffering from PTSD and should be treated, and if it means sick leave, I'm sure that would affect your pension, and the leave you're on, now."

"Terminal leave. Yes, normally if a soldier on such leave needs medical attention, she or he should go to the nearest military base. Because I'm pregnant, I was referred to a civilian doctor. I called them before I left the house the morning I met you."

Terminal leave. Jon hadn't called it by its proper name,

but he'd known it existed. And not from Rick, whose
interests lay in snowboarding in the winter and scuba
diving in the summer. He'd been too young to talk about
retirement.

They shouldn't be standing out here in the hot sun, but
he didn't want this conversation to continue in the rental
store, so he hurried it along. "Wouldn't certain kinds of
treatment affect your terminal leave?"

"Only if I require hospitalization," she answered ab-
sently, turning back to face the door.

He leaned closer, his brown, callused hand stopping
her from entering. "Regardless, you should call Veterans
Affairs. You need care, Sylvie, and they're obligated to
help you."

The urge to pull her into his arms grew, swelling until
it hurt, and he battled it with the determination he usually
reserved for difficult, dangerous shifts.

She peered up at him with a turbulent mix of suspicion
and hunger in her brilliant green eyes. When she blinked,
the expression melted into a simmering pool of wariness.

But he couldn't back down now, even if he wanted to.
"Call Veterans Affairs, Sylvie. Or I'll call them for
you."

To ease the bullying manner, he reached out and
touched her cheek, his fingers curling inward to allow his
rough knuckles to follow the line of her jaw. Her eyelids
drifted shut, only briefly. Lust exploded in him, but he
forced it way down where the burn wouldn't torment
him. He should be enjoying this private victory, instead
of holding himself in check. The smugness will have to
wait until later.

Sylvie blinked again, slowly, with precision. Her expression shifted infinitesimally. "I'll call them on Monday, on one condition. That you take me to the dinner
and auction."

Chapter 11

Another surprise. He had to get back to the real world, where every day he laid his life on the line, and the edge of danger kept him sharp in Canada's biggest city. Here he'd let himself slip if Sylvie could trick him so easily.

"Deal." What else could he say? It was only a dinner and auction in return for Sylvie's—and her unborn child's—well-being.

He could manage one short evening out with Sylvie.

He could do that, couldn't he?

On Monday Jon waited until the other men had left the supper table before he asked Sylvie the question that had nagged at him all day. "Did you call?"

"Yes." Apart from a grimace when she turned, she said nothing else.

"Good," he answered crisply. "What did they say?"

She stayed focused on the sink. "They want to interview me, and to arrange for one of their doctors to check me out. Because I'm pregnant, they're going to send one down from Edmonton. He'll examine me at the clinic.''

What she said made sense. Edmonton was home to a large military base.

''They're sending me some forms to fill out ahead of time and will arrange for an advocate to interview me. They believe there could be some compensation for me, but they didn't say what it could be.''

He blew out a sigh of relief, but she interrupted it.

''I still don't know what they can do, but I have to say that they sounded helpful on the phone. I don't want to do this for money or anything. I just want to…feel better.''

''You will.'' It was all working out well. He'd be able to leave with a clear conscience, hopefully returning in midwinter to meet his nephew or niece.

Those neat plans were all for the best. He honestly believed that.

Not sharing Jon's optimism, Sylvie watched him walk toward the campground, probably heading to the rec building to help Lawrence with some minor repairs to the door that they hadn't managed to complete earlier.

Post-traumatic stress disorder wasn't something the military accepted at the drop of a hat, and if they found out that the incident that caused it had also led to her present condition…

And Jon found out, too…

She refused to speculate any further. She'd called Veterans Affairs to please Jon. If something came of it, then she'd deal with that matter when it arose.

Jon did a double take when Sylvie slipped into the living room that Friday night. All he'd ever seen her in was jeans and loose shirts.

No, that wasn't true. He'd seen her in that long night-gown of hers, with the dipping collar and wide, flowing length.

And he'd seen her without it.

But still, the thing she wrapped herself in that night didn't compare with this outfit.

A silvery peasant-style top swept low and nearly rode off her left shoulder. When she turned, he spied the clear plastic strap of her bra. And the press of her cleavage that grew more potent each day. Her skirt waved and danced as she walked toward him, each forward thrust of her legs swirling the dark, shiny material out and around her calves. His gaze settled somewhere between her lush breasts and smooth ankles. Somewhere under her long top and swish of a light shawl, her baby lay hidden.

Rick's baby.

Sweat beaded on Jon's forehead. This was wrong. So wrong it rang out loud and clear in his head, but hell, he didn't want to listen to that damn stupid noise.

Besides, if he turned tail and convinced Sylvie he couldn't take her to the auction—say a sudden summer flu—what did he have to look forward to?

All of his options paled when he caught the shy excitement lighting Sylvie's eyes. She wanted this evening out, and after all she'd been through, she deserved it.

He only hoped he could get through the evening without touching her, because he knew exactly, thanks to the Tuesday-night classes, when he'd rubbed her back and touched her in places he shouldn't, how smooth and sensual she felt. And how his body and soul responded to her.

He couldn't let this get out of hand. Sylvie wasn't in any position to check her feelings, and damn it, after all she'd been through she shouldn't have to.

He set his jaw, knowing he had to be tough for both of them. He'd be leaving for Toronto soon enough and didn't want to return home with an ache in his heart rivaling the one he'd felt when his wife walked out, suit-case in one hand, maternity magazines in the other.

As she approached, Sylvie's steps faltered slightly. "Are you all right? You don't look well."

Here was his chance, and yet his throat slammed shut, refusing to help him form a decent word.

Finally he found his voice. "I'm fine. You look nice." Was "nice" all he could come up with? "So, any idea of what's being auctioned off?"

"Besides a few electronics, some baby things, furni-ture and such. Good thing. I need everything." She peered at him, and Jon noticed how the color of her eyes had deepened and that look of pure innocence returned. "It's like I've just realized that I'm having a baby."

Her softened expression hit him square in the gut. She needed him. Maybe only for the evening and certainly not in the way he was beginning to need her. But, hell, she needed him.

Shoving aside all the suspicions he'd carried these past few months, he knew he wanted to be needed.

Hot blood pumped through him. In vain he tried to warn himself she'd asked him out only because she needed an escort. She knew she shouldn't move too much and knew he'd want to police her in light of her doctor's orders to rest. Valid reasons, yes, but still, his body didn't care. It wanted only to be near her. Even now he could feel the desire in him rising, snubbing with a surge of joy the conscience still caught within him.

The conscience *and* the suspicion. When he'd first told her he'd be sticking around for the summer, his suspi-cions had been clear and valid. Another pregnant woman in his life admitting she had secrets. Damn, how he'd wanted to bulldoze the truth from her. But she hadn't budged, and now he wasn't so sure he could strong-arm the truth from her.

He shrugged and looked away, carefully ensuring she couldn't see his eyes. "Shall we go?"

At the community hall, they found a couple of chairs near the dance-floor end of one of the long tables. Sylvie slung her shawl over one and pointed to the other side of the room. Between the tables of smaller items to be auctioned off, the larger ones stood. One was a crib.

He stared at it.

"What's wrong?" she asked.

With a blink, he looked at her. "Nothing. Just, Rick had a crib just like that one. I remember helping my mother pick it out."

She peered across the room, her expression indefinable. He saw her jaw set. "Then that's the one I should get."

Jon nodded. The crib stood white against the muted-mushroom color of the far wall. A line of baby-blue stenciling danced along the top arched rail.

The sign taped to it stated it would be auctioned off at nine-thirty sharp.

"I sent Purley over with my meal contribution earlier today. Make sure you take some scalloped potato, okay, in case nobody eats any? My father likes it, and the men will eat it, but that doesn't mean anything."

Realizing he was still standing, Jon sat across from her. "It must. I can't imagine Lawrence not making some comment if it wasn't very good. Or even Purley for that matter."

"I'm a hothead, remember? They don't care to cross me." A hint of bitterness scraped through her voice.

Jon studied her for a moment. "I think your ranch hands know you but aren't intimidated by you."

She smiled slightly. "Is that so, Sigmund Freud? Any more insight into my cooking?"

He ignored the growing crowd around them, and spoke the thoughts he'd considered since reading the pamphlet, uncensored. "It's time to stop worrying about what others think and start caring for yourself."

She blinked. He leaned across the width of the long table, the words still flowing from him. "You're also suffering from survivor's guilt. Like I said, you're letting emotions get the better of you. Right now you're only responsible for yourself and the baby. No one else. Not even me."

She paled and bit her lip. Had he gone too far with his unchecked words? After a pause that drifted on, she spoke, her voice soft yet full of emotion. "The doctor mentioned that, but—" To anyone else here, her expression showed only cool reserve, a woman fully in control. Yet her eyes, limpid and dark, were filled with remorse. His gaze dropped to her hands, where she'd begun to rub fresh goose bumps on her arms. "You're right. I don't want to be sidetracked by anything."

He looked to the buffet table. There. He'd cut the tie between them. Subtly, but he'd cut it just the same. "I'm sure there won't be any scalloped potato left by the time we get there."

She smiled. "What do you mean, by the time we get there? Don't you know pregnant women get hungry?"

They weren't the first in line, but Jon noticed no one had yet to sample her scalloped potato, so he took a generous heaping. The smile he caught from Sylvie glowed with gratitude.

* * *

The bidding on the crib started out reasonably. One hundred dollars. Well within her budget, Sylvie noted gratefully. She'd never had to consider the cost of things before. The pay that accompanied her rank, coupled with the lack of any dependents, made it easy for her to afford whatever she'd wanted.

But nowadays she had only her pension and a ranch-campground that would break even in the fall but not before she sent some of her herd to slaughter. She'd used her own savings to rent the come-along and jacks that they would need to straighten the line shack. She had to start being frugal.

"Two hundred!"

Sylvie jerked her head around. Billy Shoemaker, a young hotshot car dealer with more money than brains, held up his numbered card. Billy's girlfriend, a mother twice over, was pregnant again, but from what Marg told her, she wanted to redo the nursery. Something to keep her busy in case the kids didn't.

She swallowed and lifted her card. "Two twenty-five."

"Three hundred!"

Good grief, what was Billy doing? Playing philanthropist to drum up more business for himself?

Sagging, she dropped her card into her decreasing lap. She'd find another crib someplace else.

"Five hundred." Jon scooped up the card and held it high for the auctioneer to see. Then turned to glare at Billy Shoemaker.

Panic flared in her. "What are you doing? I can't afford that much!"

"But I can. And I'm not letting junior-car-dealer-of-the-year steal that crib from you. He needs to save his money for those big buck suits he wears selling tractors to cash-strapped farmers.'' He grinned boldly at her.

Her breath left her in one short burst at the thought of his gorgeous smile. She had never seen him so cheerful yet determined.

''Sold!'' The auctioneer wasted no time. He'd barely given Billy Shoemaker a chance before he banged his gavel down.

Sylvie's heart pounded. She wanted to hug Jon. No, she wanted to climb into his lap and kiss him hard on his grinning mouth until they were both senseless. Right that very minute.

But the knot in her stomach tightened and she reined in the lustful thought. She couldn't be falling for Jon, could she? The emotion of the moment only sidetracked her. Emotion and a heck of a lot of guilt, especially if she considered Jon's words earlier this evening about how she should be taking care of herself and not let emotions get the better of her.

So true. The last time—the only time—she'd let emotions take over her sensibility, a Cahill man had died.

She wouldn't—God, she couldn't—risk Jon. Not even one scrap of him.

Her hand strayed to her growing abdomen. Jon caught the movement.

''Thank you,'' she whispered.

His smile slipped away, leaving a residue of what seemed like her own hungry emotions. No, it was just a reflection in his eyes. ''You're welcome,'' he finally answered. ''You look a bit done in. Want to call it a night? Or is there something else you'd like to bid on?''

The desire to kiss him flared again. She shook her head to throw it off. ''Nothing. If I win anything in the silent auction, they'll call me.''

Jon leaned behind her to sweep her shawl over her shoulders. His fingers rested on her arm for a moment. Only a shawl as thin as this one would permit his bold heat to penetrate her. She tugged the light material together, and he released his hand. Her voice cracked. ''I'm ready.''

They sat there a moment. She was waiting for him to move. Around them swirled the auctioneer's swift calling. Earlier Jon had dragged his seat around the table, closer to her, but he didn't move.

His eyes were a different color. Not the piercing blue she'd learned to fortify herself against, but darker, aching, *hungrier.*

Not for her. Please not for her. They'd just bought a crib for her baby. The one that was, right now, fluttering a wild, swift rhythm against her full bladder, in time with the auctioneer's vocal cadence.

He couldn't be considering sex with her. He *wouldn't* be if he knew the truth. She'd been a coward that night in the truck, abandoning her training and her common sense.

Jon knew none of that. She could tell in his eyes the only thing he knew.

He knew he wanted her.

And she knew she wanted him.

Jon's pants dug into his groin. He'd tried several methods to ease the discomfort, walking out to bring the truck around to the back of the hall, loading the crib with one of the volunteer's help. Even in the truck driving home, he shifted a lot. Nothing worked.

Sylvie's face had glowed when he'd secured the top bid. She'd kept staring at him with eyes a melting pot of feelings.

He had to get them home before he found it impossible to drive and was forced to pull over and finish what his mind kept previewing over and over.

"What are you thinking about? Not the money, I hope. I can pay you—"

"The crib is yours, Sylvie. A gift." She didn't need to know his thoughts. They'd scare her. Heaven knew they were scaring the hell out of him.

He forced a harsh review of why he was really here. Because she knew Rick's last moments. Because she knew Rick better than he did.

Because she kept secrets.

That's why he was here. Nothing else, especially not because he was beginning to give a damn about Sylvie, when he shouldn't.

"You're so quiet," she said.

A blurring answer slid from his lips. "Just sorting out my mental agenda. It won't be long before I have to head back to Toronto. I've really never had a job where I didn't work shift and I actually lived where I worked."

"Oh." She paused, leaving him to berate himself for the cold answer.

She stared out the passenger window. "And you're finding it stressful?"

He laughed, knowing the laugh came out forced. "No, the opposite. I haven't had to think much. You and Lawrence make the decisions. Purley, Michael and I do the work. It's a pretty simple life-style."

"Oh." Her expression slackened. "I imagine it's boring compared to the excitement of fighting crime in a big city. Don't you cops get high on all the adrenaline?"

By this time, they'd reached the ranch's driveway. "What have you been watching on TV?"

She rolled her eyes. "I spent five months in Bosnia. Since then, I've been running a ranch and a campground. I don't have time to watch TV. And I haven't read any of those cop books, either." She lifted her shoulders indifferently. "There's got to be some reason for guys like you to become police officers. You wouldn't be the first guy who lived on adrenaline. I know some soldiers like that."

"Did Rick?"

She waited until he'd shut off the motor and removed the keys before she unbuckled her seat belt. When she spoke, her voice had turned softer. "You didn't really know Rick, did you?"

He wanted to swear, but caught the nasty word in time. No, he didn't know Rick. Sure they talked, e-mailed, tried to squeeze Christmas vacations in once in a while, but with no parents to meet with every summer, they didn't…couldn't find the time or space. Sylvie knew Rick. Intimately. Jon forced his mind to acknowledge the gut-wrenching fact that his baby brother had had something he couldn't have.

Knowing Sylvie intimately wouldn't be ethical. And above all else, the man inside of him, the cop, the uncle of her baby, they *all* wanted to be ethical, damn it. "We tried to get together when we could."

"But Rick and I spent Christmas in Bosnia," she finished for him.

Yeah. When Rick had called to tell him he was going to Bosnia, and would be there until the spring, Jon knew the chances of an unmarried, orphaned soldier getting leave at Christmas would be slim. Many others had families, small kids who deserved to have their moms and dads there when they opened their presents.

Jon looked over to her, his heart thumping hard inside of him. "So, what did Rick do at Christmas?"

"Worked. We both did. We'd had rations delivered the day before along with some care packages from the Legion and the Red Cross. We wanted to make sure that everyone had a present to open on Christmas Day." Her voice cracked, and she blinked several times.

His own eyes burned. He'd sent Rick a small package, at the prompting of a female officer who'd heard about him. The parcel hadn't been much, some of Rick's favorite chocolate bars and a sweatshirt that bore the Toronto Police logo. The female officer donated a magazine, boxer briefs, socks and some microwave popcorn. He'd been a bit embarrassed that he hadn't thought of those.

His throat hurt. "Did he get my parcel?"

Sylvie frowned. "Yes. He wore a sweatshirt with a cop logo on it Christmas Day. Someone had sent him a box of microwave popcorn, which we ate Christmas evening after I did guard duty. It's traditional for all of the officers and sergeants to do the duties that day, so the junior ranks could enjoy Christmas. It was quiet all over camp, so we just kicked back at the QM stores and had a few beers."

One question lingered on Jon's mind. Did Rick enjoy Christmas with Sylvie making love?

Did Jon want to know that?

The crib looked beautiful, despite sitting square in the middle of the room, bare as desert bones, surrounded by half-unpacked boxes.

Sylvie swallowed the lump in her throat. She was going to have the most beautiful baby in the world, she just knew it, and in a few months he'd be sleeping here, waiting to turn his mother's already crazy world upside down.

As if agreeing, he moved against her, grazing one of her sore muscles.

"Ooh." She gently rubbed the area and smiled a watery smile at Jon. "He's stretching. Must be doing warm-ups for tonight's calisthenics."

Jon stared down at her hand, his expression hungry.

"Here." Gee, did she have to sound so breathy and shy? "Feel him. I think of him as a boy and, let me say, he's an active one." She grabbed a fistful of her thin shirt. She'd been ready to pull it up when she stopped.

No. Not after what she'd done in her office. Exposing her belly didn't feel proper all of a sudden. And yet Jon's expression remained riveted to her.

She stretched the shirt taut across her belly and pressed his hand heavily against her skin.

He was warm. She hadn't been cool since she fainted in June, but Jon, he was warmer than she was.

And so close. He'd stepped into her comfort zone with his palm flat over the thin material of her shirt. She glanced over to the window, thankful she'd pulled the curtains closed earlier in the evening.

She turned her attention back to Jon. He watched her closely, his fingers pushing ever so carefully against the tiny hardness, a smile flitting over his smooth lips when the baby moved again. She caught his throat bobbing, his eyes blink, once, three, four times—too rapidly for her to count.

His gaze slipped from her face, down her neck, to settle for too short a time on her blossoming cleavage. Her breasts answered in that burning way she'd begun to realize always happened when Jon cast an intense, smoldering expression her way.

Below, his fingers were splayed across her belly. When they roamed down, the hem of the blouse fell out and over his hand, as if it recognized the extent of the intimacy and insisted on offering the privacy Jon's touch deserved.

His hand moved upward.

She shifted closer to him, shocking herself when her hips thrust themselves toward him, so close she couldn't mistake the hard scrape of his jeans on her belly.

She was crazy to do this, yet…

Jon moved his hand upward. When he reached the warm lace that covered her breasts, he stopped. "Sylvie—"

"No." She looked directly into his eyes. "Don't tell me how wrong this is." With her knees rubbery and threatening to buckle at any second, she gripped Jon's thick biceps, appreciating how strong he was, how big, how much his own hand had begun to shake slightly against her breasts. How close he was to her racing heart.

His eyes darkened and he wet his lips. "I wasn't planning to say anything of the kind. But I can't keep my hand still much longer. I want you to tell me you're comfortable with this."

"Comfortable?" She let a breathy giggle escape. "I wouldn't call what I'm feeling 'comfortable.'"

She felt his jeans press into her and she knew then that her words had aroused him. Good. A surge of control shot through her. Jon had dictated much of her life in the past few weeks, and she'd had no choice in obeying his common sense. But now he'd relinquished control to her, and the heady lure of it pulled her in.

She could do something she'd ached to do for weeks.

Make love to Jonathon Cahill. Before he exercised that common sense of his and stopped them both.

Chapter 12

Jon's hand shook like those aspen trees around the campground when the hot, dry winds blew down on them. Any words he'd had now lodged in his throat. What had he planned to say? That he didn't want to make love to her?

Nothing could be further from the truth.

Her hand settled on his hip, her belly pressing against the more obvious answer to his internal question.

Jon had never made love to a pregnant woman before. His ex-wife and he had stopped touching each other months before she announced she was pregnant and leaving.

Hell, he'd be leaving soon himself.

Without the truth about Rick? Could he? The answer didn't seem to want to form in his mind. Instead, another clear question focused there. Did those answers even matter anymore?

His hand, impatient at the wait, roamed up to explore

the lacy, well-filled bra. Her nipple prodded bluntly against the tips of his fingers. He nearly burst with need, right then and there.

She ground herself into his arousal, slowly, with the determination she was noted for.

Sweat trickled down his back. He had to get them onto the bed, and soon. Yet Sylvie appeared in no rush to move anywhere, except closer to him. And the sweet, delaying pleasure tempted him.

She was in control, not him. Holy cow, he'd never been seduced before. Some of the women he'd known intimately may have suggested the seduction, but he always, *always* took over, fully in charge and fully satisfied at the end. And he always made sure they were, too.

Sylvie had other plans, however, and his body willingly accommodated the change in the status quo.

Her head tilted back and her eyelids drifted shut and she stretched upward to meet his lips.

He stole the moment to study her, until soft, slightly pouty lips swept across his. Her tongue danced across the edge of his teeth, asking for an invitation to enter. She tasted like the cheesecake she'd had for dessert. Rich, creamy sweetness with a tang.

Abruptly she ended the light brush of a kiss. With a slight smile she led him into her bedroom. His hand, now free from her blouse, felt cold and decidedly empty.

The bedroom door clicked shut behind him. In front, Sylvie drew her blouse over her head. He watched as it floated to the floor. Reaching behind her, she released her bra and it followed her blouse downward. Then, for a flash, hesitation—and that damned strange innocence— swept across her features.

"What's wrong?"

"Seems the last time I did this—" she paused "—you flatly refused me."

What was wrong with him? "You were standing in front of the window. Besides, you stripped off for a different reason, didn't you?"

"I wanted to feel something." Her tongue flicked over her lips. "Anything but despair."

She waited. Mesmerized by the rhythmic rise and fall of her bare breasts, he could hardly find his raspy voice. "And tonight? Do you still feel the same way?"

Her sigh ended in a laugh. Then, with eyelids half-shut, she shook her head. "Not in the least. But I do want something. Someone. You."

Coming up closer to him, she reached for his hair, brushing back the one lock that always fell forward. Her breasts lifted up with her arm to barely touch his shirt. He shut his eyes to the straining need inside of him. She had no idea of the sweet torture she inflicted.

He fumbled with the waistband of her skirt, and once he'd slipped it over her rounded belly, it collapsed to the floor. The urge to drop to his knees and press his mouth against her bare skin swelled in him, but he reined it in hard. It was too soon.

A pair of high-cut black panties, similar to the snowy ones, curved up over her hips.

She'd begun to unfasten his shirt. Good thing, he admitted to himself. He might not have managed the buttons. He would rather have torn the shirt apart than have fumbled with them. The need inside of him tightened, like a coil spring compressed beyond measure, waiting to explode.

Once she'd freed him of his shirt, she focused on his jeans. Her slight smile hinted of how much she enjoyed the control she wielded. He was thankful for it, as well.

If not for such control, he'd have long since pressed her into her bed and thrust himself into her, with his jeans pooled at his knees. He'd have their first lovemaking over far too soon for either of them.

He stepped out of the jeans—and the boxers she'd just shoved down his legs. He expected her to study him, or stay down there, but she, with half-closed eyes, straightened and guided him to her bed. With a shy smile, she pushed him back onto the soft, enveloping duvet.

And then she crawled between his legs.

He couldn't stand much more of this torture. His breath tight in his lungs, he waited for her to...do anything to him. Instead, she hovered over the part of him that needed her the most.

"Sylvie—" He grated out the warning as he reached for her.

"Shh." She crawled up further and settled herself down on him. She still wore those insane panties! He should just rip them off....

She stilled his hand when he lifted it. Her warm breasts scrubbed his chest hair as she leaned over him.

Her kiss was featherlight, as quick as a heartbeat and bore that trademark innocence. If he didn't know better—

"Let me do this," she whispered. "I've behaved myself for weeks for you and this baby. I've drunk all that milk you poured for me at each meal. I've hardly lifted a finger and I don't do anything for myself anymore. I feel like I'm not myself half the time and the other half I feel like a breeding cow. I don't want to talk or think or be anyone other than *this* person I am now. So please," she brushed her lips over his again. "Please let me be this person now. Just for tonight."

He groaned, his length sandwiched between them. The person she was right now was driving him crazy.

"Give me a little control, Jon?"

He shut his eyes. She sounded like a curious, exotic mix of shy virgin and steamy siren.

"Yeah." What the hell else could he say?

She climbed off the bed and—his breath caught—out of her panties.

He could barely focus his vision. How could it be that he needed her so badly? What had happened to all those carefully erected walls of defense? Where was that insistent voice reminding him she had secrets? And a past? Besides, he was a cop with a failed marriage behind him, too wrapped up with his own work to bother with the long-term commitment he knew they would both expect...

And what the hell happened to the respect he carried for Rick?

She settled down on him, warming him intimately with her own snug heat. And she watched him, too, tiny cries drifting out of her parted lips every so often, all the while controlling their satisfaction, with little wasted energy.

He loved her.

The second the realization hit him, a potent curse exploded in his mouth. He shut his eyes, clamped down his jaw and kept the blasted word captive, not wanting to ruin the moment they were sharing, the increasingly dynamic, rising moment.

The rhythm she'd started grew stronger, faster, wilder.

When he felt her shudder, he opened his eyes. She collapsed on him, her breasts, now moistened with perspiration, slamming into his own damp chest.

What were they doing? She was carrying Rick's baby and he was having sex with her.

No! Not sex. This wasn't just some quickie to top off some evening with a woman he barely knew.

This was Sylvie, the woman he loved.

Now, as she buried her head in the hot hollow of his throat, he knew that, regardless of the fact she belonged to Rick and not him, he loved her more than he loved himself.

She tightened around him, pulling him into her, holding him with everything she had.

And he found his own shuddering, overwhelming release deep inside of her.

They lay there, still joined, still drifting down from someplace as close to heaven as he'd ever get. At least, he drifted. Her whimpering moments ago had put her somewhere up there, too, he wagered.

He should regret this. He should be lifting her off him and apologizing profusely for even wanting to make love to her. But he couldn't. Instead, as the minutes passed, he grew again inside of her.

And judging by the subtle grindings she'd started with her slick body, she wanted what he needed.

Or did she?

He checked his urges tightly, focusing on her wet face as it lay buried in his neck.

Why the hell was she crying?

Chapter 13

She was still thinking of her foolish tears from last night when she spotted the staff car gliding smoothly in over the potholes in her driveway. The damn tears still baffled her, but she'd managed to sweep them away before Jon noticed them.

Just the release of stress, she told herself, the overwhelming emotions pouring out of her when she finally admitted to herself that she loved Jon Cahill.

Even now, in her office, the love still struck her hard in the center of her chest.

But she could never tell him. He'd be leaving to return to his own life in Toronto and he wouldn't want to be burdened with the knowledge she'd fallen for him. He had a right to see his brother's child, and she wouldn't want him troubled by her feelings during any future visits.

The papers and invoices on her desk fluttered in the breeze that slipped in behind her.

She'd need every last scrap of self-control the military had taught her, but she'd do it. She'd keep her feelings, and her secrets, safely hidden.

Her hand strayed to her stomach. Life had never been so complicated, so difficult to sort out. Carrying one man's child, in love with another. Both men brothers yet worlds apart, pulling her taut like a rubber band ready to break. She couldn't think of one without thinking of the other, and she needed to catalog her feelings, but they seemed to ruffle around her like the papers on her desk.

The sound of the military vehicle penetrated her office like an armored tank.

She stood and slipped closer to the window. Hot summer air flowed in, hitting her through the ugly maternity pants she'd been forced to wear.

A soldier in combat fatigues climbed out. *Oh, no.* Major Tirouski. With a briefcase.

Despite the hot air, she shivered. The man could drop the ambient temperature ten degrees with just his presence.

After surveying the grounds a moment with what Sylvie could imagine was a cool, methodical stare, he walked over to Michael, who had just thrown a small square haybale to the llamas.

The major's voice filtered over to her. "I'm looking for Mr. Cahill. Do you know where I can find him?"

Sylvie shrank away from the window, her heart pounding. She hadn't really expected the officer. Sometimes the local militia would drop by to request permission to cross her land at the northern edge, but she'd be a fool to hope for something so benign from the major.

He was here to give Jon the final report on Rick's death.

The full autopsy, also? A heartrending list, itemized as

she might have done with the well-stocked shelves of her unit's QM?

Would the autopsy also include the fact he'd had sexual intercourse hours before his death? Could a medical examiner find such evidence on a man, the way they could with a woman? Would he even think to look for it?

With eyes shut tight, she prayed they couldn't.

She should close the window. Slam it hard and shove all such guilty speculation from her mind.

Michael called out across the front yard, toward the campground office, and a moment later Jon strode across the dusty driveway.

She'd barely spoken to Jon at breakfast, choosing instead to ply Purley and Michael with endless toast and coffee, while answering Lawrence's questions about some chores at the campground side of the business. Throughout the meal, she'd forced her eyes to stop roaming toward Jon, where he sat wordlessly eating his bacon and eggs.

No one commented on the fact that Jon hadn't returned to the bunkhouse the night before.

And today she hadn't expected him to be so handy, but then again, she had mentioned that the window in the campground office needed adjusting.

She couldn't move. The breeze had waned, and her feet, now ice, froze to the floor. Her hands clutching the sill, she watched Jon shove out his hand to welcome the officer. Their voices cut through the dry air with perfect clarity.

"Mr. Cahill, as you know, I'm the liaison officer assigned to the committee investigating your brother's death. Is there anywhere private we can talk?"

Jon swung around, peering at the house. At her window.

Their gazes locked.

And her heart stopped.

With his Stetson on, she could only guess his expression. But regardless of his hidden thoughts, his gaze lingered on her, like his hands had last night, when he'd decided he'd had enough of lying there while she made love to him. When he'd rolled them both over and pinned her to the bed with a consuming gaze and a mouth that knew how to love a woman.

Would he ask her to join him?

Please, no. Please leave me out of this.

Shocked by her own cowardice, she blinked several times. The wind picked up again, and she had to make a conscious effort to inhale. Outside, Jon broke the eye contact and removed his Stetson. Then, as he wiped his brow, he turned his attention to the officer and indicated the porch ahead.

Oh, no. Please not so close.

"Warm today, isn't it?" The officer made small talk as they made their way up the steps. Even though they were out of view, their voices grew louder. The porch didn't wrap around to include her office, but Sylvie knew she was a mere yard from where the two men stood.

Oh, Lord, she didn't want to hear this conversation, and it wasn't because it was Jon's private moment, the truth he'd been seeking to finally bury Rick in his heart.

She was a coward. Just as she'd been that night in the truck. A coward, bent on easing her own fear. And killing Rick in the process.

"So, let's cut to the chase, shall we?" Jon's voice penetrated the office. "All I was told was that Rick probably died from his injuries. Are you going to tell me more?''

"Mr. Cahill, let me first say that the Armed Forces deeply regrets Private Cahill's death. His loss has been felt not just in his unit, but throughout the entire military."

Such lip service nearly always accompanied bad news. She sank onto her chair, too frightened to slam shut the window, hating that the major hadn't followed Jon's gaze and seen her there and suggested a more private spot.

Do your job and leave, Major.

There was a rustling of paper, the officer having pulled some documents from his briefcase. Sylvie waited, knowing that Jon had chosen the porch because she was so close, listening, however unwillingly.

And if she left the office, she'd be spotted through the window of the front door.

She was trapped. Just as she'd been in her supply truck that night.

The major cleared his throat. "Before we go over this report, I'd like to explain what exactly we investigated and how."

"How did my brother die?"

"Mr. Cahill, the autopsy report is—"

"Major, my brother was attacked. I want to know by whom and what this government has done about it."

A distinctive pause followed. "Mr. Cahill, this ranch belongs to Warrant Officer Mitchell, doesn't it?"

Jon's voice tightened. "Does that present a problem to you, Major?"

"Has she discussed the incident with you?"

"Is that what the military is calling Rick's death?"

Sylvie shut her eyes. Not since Major Tirouski had come weeks ago to remind her she was obligated by law to stay silent, had she felt her heart wrench so much. An incident? Rick deserved more. So did Jon.

The major resumed talking. "Mr. Cahill, we investigated all aspects of the incident. For ease of explanation, I can go through the investigation in a chronological manner."

What was Jon doing? Suddenly the urge to see him, hold him, overpowered the horrible cowardice she'd felt earlier. She pushed herself to standing and hurried from her office. A quick turn on her heel and she was at the front door.

Jon glanced up, their gazes colliding through the window of the door. He sat on one of her wicker chairs, facing the house, while the major sat on another chair with his back to her, completely unaware of her presence.

For the moment the officer skimmed the documents, and Jon's frustrated expression hardened.

Sylvie reached out to touch the door. Quickly Jon shook his head, his mouth forming a short, cold *no*.

He didn't want her there? She swallowed, ready to ignore his silent request, just as he mouthed something else. *Back off!*

What? For a flash, she thought he'd cursed her, but then the actual words settled silently into her. How could he so rudely tell her to leave? Reluctantly, she melted into the shadows of the hallway. Though muted by the insulated door, she could still hear Major Tirouski's booming voice.

"We began an initial investigation immediately upon Private Cahill's arrival at the camp. Here is a copy of the initial investigation, and a partial transcript of military police communications—"

"Partial? Why partial?"

"Some of their conversation is considered sensitive in nature. I'm sure as a police officer, you understand."

Sylvie waited for Jon's answer, but it didn't come. Yes, he'd understand, but he'd hate it.

The major must have sensed something. "Mr. Cahill, you have to understand we can't give you a full report."

There was more rustling of paper. The creak of the porch floor betrayed the fact Jon had stood. "Major, what's the point of giving me a report at all? Is this supposed to make me feel better? My brother's dead. Some coward killed him. What has been done to find that person and bring him to justice?"

"You must understand—"

"No, Major, you understand. I want to find that person myself and wring his neck. I've wanted nothing more since I received that phone call from the army chaplain that night. What has been done to find that person?"

"Mr. Cahill," the major began again. "You must understand that your brother was a soldier in a war zone—"

"The war was supposed to be over, Major."

"Yes, Mr. Cahill. Your brother was part of the Sustainment Force to make peace possible, but sometimes peace takes time." More rustling of papers followed the major's tight words. Sylvie gripped the door to the kitchen, feeling her stomach heave.

Jon's voice grew louder. "Major, I don't see anywhere, the actual events that led up to Rick's death. Was he able to defend himself? What kind of protection did he have?"

"Here is a list of equipment your brother was wearing when he was brought in. You can see he had on all his personal protective equipment."

"Where's the ballistics report? He'd been shot, but when I spoke to the pathologist in Toronto who per-

formed the autopsy, he didn't extract any bullets or shrap-
nel.''

''The unit's surgeon performed emergency surgery on
Private Cahill—''

''Damn it, his name was Rick!''

The major's voice dropped, moderating with contri-
tion. ''Yes, of course. As I was saying, the surgeon tried
to keep him alive, but he'd gone too long without medical
attention.''

''He had survived the night with Sylvie.''

She could feel the air throughout the house chill. Finally, in a quieter, lower tone, the major said, ''Mr. Cahill, have you been speaking to Warrant Officer Mitchell
on this matter?''

Again, maddening silence. Finally, Jon spoke. ''Major,
is there some reason why I *should* speak to Sylvie...*on
this matter?* For something not mentioned in this...fil-
tered report?''

The major's tone turned smooth, more patient. ''Warrant Officer Mitchell cannot give you an accurate ac-
count. She was under duress during the time and did not
handle your brother's death very well. I would probably
discount what she might have to say about your brother,
apart from the fact that he was a good soldier. She had
to speak to a counselor several times, and in fact, we
have already asked Veterans Affairs—''

Sylvie couldn't listen to any more. She wasn't on the
brink of insanity. The counseling sessions had ceased
when she left the military. Simple as that. And if the
major had somehow got wind of her request to Veterans
Affairs...

She may have acted cowardly the night Rick died, but
not now. Not when Jon needed her. He needed her and
suddenly she needed to hold him. Tightly.

But just as she stepped into the hallway, she remembered Tirouski's last visit. And the nondisclosure agreement she'd signed, and her training tugged her back. Surely they knew the truth she'd already guessed—

"Sylvie?"

She spun around with a start. Lawrence stood there, his thick gray brows knitted into one tight line. He and Purley were to straighten the line shack this afternoon. What was he doing here? "Is there something wrong?"

He shook his head, all the while peering over her shoulder with unabashed interest. "Nothing. The jacks we rented are too small. I sent Purley into town to replace them. The line shack will have to wait another day. Who's the soldier out there?"

She glanced back to the front door, seeing Major Tirouski's shoulder flashes. The rank displayed on them was clearly visible. When Lawrence touched her arm, she jumped again.

Oh, Lord in Heaven, she could hardly breathe. Her voice dropped. "He's here to deliver the report on Rick's death."

Lawrence's mouth formed a thin line. "And it isn't good news, is it?"

"I didn't mean to eavesdrop. I was in the office and Jon knew it. He even brought the major over to the porch on purpose. I think he wanted me to overhear it. I should have gone out—"

"No. If Jon had wanted you out there, he would have asked you to come out on the porch."

"But he knew I could hear."

"Is that officer the same gentleman who was here a few weeks ago?"

She hadn't expected Lawrence to know that Tirouski had visited. But then, not much got by him. "Yes, and I know he's just doing his job, but he wasn't that much of a gentleman the last time he came.''

"That explains why Jon might want you to overhear but not go out. And I agree. You shouldn't go out there.'' Lawrence's glance to her growing abdomen was quick but unmistakable.

She touched her belly. Right now it was the only part of her that felt warm. Lawrence was right. She couldn't possibly go out to the porch.

A gentle touch on her arm made her turn. When she looked up into Lawrence's craggy face, she saw only compassion. "Is there something Jon deserves to know that isn't in that report?'' he asked her.

She sighed. Lawrence knew her so well. Her voice cracked when she spoke. "I've signed a nondisclosure agreement. It's a gag order—''

"Really?'' Lawrence's tone was dry. "I had no idea you had military secrets.''

She rolled her eyes. "Everyone signs one so the military can try to prevent you from going to the media or writing a best-selling tell-all book on them.''

"So there is something Jon should know.''

She quickly swiped her hand across her eyes and down her face. "It won't bring Rick back. We can't change anything. And these past few weeks…'' Where could she start? "Well, I've been arguing with myself whether I should tell Jon anything.''

"Like what?''

She turned in time to catch Jon walking the major to his staff car. He held his shoulders straight as a board and her heart wrenched at the sight of him.

Jon hadn't got his closure after all.

She finally spoke. "Everything.'' *Even that I killed Rick,* she wanted to add.

Lawrence peered over her shoulder. "Nothing stopping you now."

She turned to see the staff car disappear down the long, dusty drive. Jon turned, his head down, his steps achingly slow.

She suppressed the urge to run out and catch him in a hard hug, one meant to comfort. "It's not what Jon wants to hear."

"How so?"

"I let my emotions get the better of me and neglected my duty."

"Jon can handle that."

Lawrence didn't understand. "No, Rick was—" She stopped, and the idea of unburdening herself reared its ugly head again. Beyond, where Jon stood, the dust left by the staff car dissipated. She couldn't unburden herself with half-truths. Jon didn't deserve that. But she couldn't be silent anymore. To hell with a court martial.

The old man frowned. "Was it Rick's own fault that he died?"

She faced Lawrence again, her jaw tight. For a long, strained minute neither said a word. Finally she threw back her shoulders. "No. It was mine, Lawrence, and it's time I paid for it."

Chapter 14

She's already started to waddle a bit, Jon noticed as Sylvie approached him. Her hips hadn't widened overly much, but her walk was as distinctively maternal as the fullness of her breasts and the small outward curve of her belly.

Whoa. He'd just finished one of the most difficult conversations of his life and still he managed to switch channels to Sylvie with disturbing ease.

It didn't seem right.

Thank the Lord she'd done as he mouthed back there. The major would have taken one look at her and known her condition. And if the man had any kids, he might have easily guessed how far along she was.

And no way in hell did he want Tirouski to know any damn thing about Sylvie.

The protective instinct hit him with full, hard force. Even though the situation had never formed, he couldn't stop the defensive tide growing in him.

Sylvie's face pinched into a frown and she stopped just at the parched edge of the grass. One hand settled on her belly, the other crept to her breasts, a gesture that stirred the memory of last night.

She'd moved her hands to a similar position last night, during their—was it their third time!—lovemaking. What she'd done had been more stimulating, and even the mere memory fanned the embers inside of him, despite the disappointing news the major had grimly delivered.

He shoved his hat up on his head, feeling the heat radiate upward from the bone-dry driveway. What the hell was he thinking? Here, he'd been told of Rick's "accidental death," given a laughably censored report, and the only thing on his mind was what Sylvie could do with her ripening body?

He should be focused on Rick's death. He should be doing…something more. Writing letters. Getting the government to recognize the potential dangers facing their soldiers. They should tell the whole truth to military families and taxpayers who held the mistaken belief that stability existed all over Bosnia and that their soldiers were safe. And he should be focusing on the fact that the cowardly bastard who'd killed Rick still walked free, just as the man who'd killed his father walked free.

But he couldn't. Sylvie still lingered on his mind. He loved her, yet they seemed as far apart as possible. How could there be any chance for happiness together? She wanted to put Bosnia in the past and she should. He couldn't even open his brother's barrack boxes yet. She had secrets, and he wanted to force them out of her.

He plodded over to where she stood. Her eyes glistened with sympathy, and he ached to pull her into a hard embrace.

"What did the report say?" she asked.

He steered her inside, through the dark house to the living room. Not her bedroom. Not anyplace private. When they stopped in the middle of the room, he heard the kitchen door slam shut. Hoping it was Lawrence or the ·other two, and that they were staying, he held his breath. But off behind the house, a truck started and he knew Sylvie and he were alone.

He wasn't sure if it was a good thing or not. To kill the ticking moments, he returned to the porch to collect the papers he'd been given.

"Major Tirouski should never have wasted his time." He slammed the front door shut. "The report was so heavily censored, it shouldn't even have been written."

Why the hell couldn't the major have forgotten them? The last few weeks had been the best Sylvie had ever experienced. And last night she'd realized she could be more than the shell she'd become during those last few days in Bosnia. And here at home.

And Jon, too, had begun to enjoy the summer. She was sure of that. Yes, the work was long and hard, but in the evenings they'd done up the dishes together, talking about life at the ranch or life in Toronto, filling the quiet evenings with shared stories of the more colorful moments in their lives and careers.

She had to tell him the truth. Oh God, he deserved so much more than the ridiculous report he'd just thrown down on the coffee table. The papers had spilled apart, all three pages, neatly formatted, and, she caught the words *apologize, regrets, understanding* mocking them.

She drew in a deep breath. "Jon, there is more to Rick's death than what they've given you. Things you deserve to know."

* * *

He couldn't believe his ears. Anger filled him as he collected the report, only to throw the damnably thin thing down. That was all he'd have of Rick's last day? Sympathy? And silence blamed on national security? And now Sylvie wanted to talk?

Hell.

A short, anxious-sounding sigh burst from Sylvie's mouth, and he shot up his head to glare at her. He didn't bother to hide his irritation. "What about the nondisclosure form you signed?"

"To hell with it." She kept on talking. "I know that the brass want this *incident* to be kept quiet. But I hated that it was all subdued. Rick deserved better. And I hated Bosnia." She rolled her eyes. "I still do. There's no good guys or bad guys over there. It's just a bunch of ethnic groups fighting. And they've been fighting for hundreds of years long before we got there. And they will long after we leave. It'll never end. They all signed this Dayton Accord, and we were over there to keep the peace, but the fighting hasn't really stopped."

Spoken like a war-weary soldier, he thought. And she was right in many ways. Sometimes he even got tired of gangs battling it out in Toronto. Sometimes he wished all of them would just kill themselves off, the lot of them, and save so many innocent lives.

But her conflict had been much worse.

She pulled air into her lungs and her tongue flicked nervously over her lips. That task done, she walked to the picture window where the lace bowed into the room, blown by the breeze. Holding his breath, Jon felt the warm wind seep into the living room.

"It was supposed to be a routine supply run. The only thing different was that this outpost had been temporarily manned by the German contingent and we were to support them for about a month. They needed rations and some paper products and some sandbags. They'd asked for more, but the captain ordered us to take just the essentials. The only thing of value that I'd taken was the office cell phone.''

She sighed. ''We didn't even have any ammo with us. Just a couple of full mags each. There was nothing worth an ambush. Nothing worth dying over. Not in the truck, and not on us.''

His hands shook and he forced them into his jeans pockets. His arms ached to hold her. She shouldn't have to relive all of this torture. Hadn't she suffered enough?

And yet…he'd waited so long for this moment. His jaw tight, he ground out, ''What happened that night?''

She toyed with the lace curtain in front of her. ''The weather was really bad. It had already delayed us once, and when we figured it was letting up, we left the base camp. We were expecting to drive all evening and spend the night at the outpost, then return the next day. But the weather just got worse.''

She took another breath. *Talk to me, Sylvie. Talk to me.*

Finally she continued. ''After we'd gone about twenty kilometers into the mountains, and made the turn we were supposed to make, the weather worsened. Rainy, slick, and the higher we climbed, the worse it got. Before long the rain had turned to sleet and then snow, and I knew something was wrong. I guess it was intuition, because there was no other reason for me to be suspicious.''

She turned and glanced at him, as if gauging his reaction so far to her words. He kept his face as neutral as possible.

''Then we drove around one hairpin turn, a really bad one, and there it was. Rocks and trees and mud all strewn over the road. A landslide, we figured. Rick barely stopped the truck in time. But as soon as we got out—'' her voice hitched up ''—a-after we got out of the truck, we realized it had been deliberately set.''

His heart punched a nasty tattoo in his throat. He tried to breathe, but the hot air in the living room turned leaden when he inhaled.

This was it.

Sylvie's hands twisted the lace into a tight knot. She was no longer looking at him but at the intricate pattern of the curtain.

He should stop this torture. Right now. But he couldn't speak.

''We'd only been standing in front of the truck for half a minute, and I'd just suggested we winch the big stuff to the side. We had a good winch on the front of the truck. We could do it. But we never had a chance.''

She swallowed. Jon stepped forward to grab her, but she stopped him with her hands, now released from their lace prison. ''They opened fire on us.''

He dropped his hands. ''Did you have your sidearm with you?''

She nodded. ''Rick had his rifle, with a round up the spout and the safety on. That's standard. I had my pistol. As soon as the first round hit the truck, I shoved Rick to the ground and covered him. Then we scrambled under the front of the truck. Rick looked at me, and I gave the order to fire back.''

''You? He had to wait for you?''

''The senior rank gives the order. It's part of the rules of engagement. I didn't even challenge first. You know, yell out who we were and to stop or we'll open fire. All that crap.''

''Why not?''

"We didn't have time. They were still firing at us. And if you're attacked so unexpectedly that challenging the enemy would endanger your life, you don't have to. We didn't know where they were. The snow was pretty heavy by that time. We couldn't see anything. But we fired off a few rounds, anyway. They kept on firing. It seemed like they were all around us."

"What happened then?"

She began to rub her arms. He couldn't imagine her cold. To him, the whole room was stifling, an inferno. She stopped rubbing after a minute. "We crawled under the truck to the back."

"Were you planning on climbing into the back of the truck?"

"Ultimately, yes. We couldn't go back into the cab. There was nowhere to drive. We couldn't see a thing. So the only safe thing to do was crawl into the back. Rick had shut off the engine and taken the keys with him. The truck would have been useless to whoever was firing on us." She stopped talking.

"What did you do next?" *Come on, Sylvie. Don't stop now. Tell me, baby. Tell me everything.*

The lace pattern had been studied enough. She looked away from both it and him. "Once we'd crawled to the back of the truck, the firing stopped." She paused. "I guess they couldn't see us anymore. I had the company cell phone with me, and while I was crouching under the driveshaft, I tried to call the captain."

"Back at camp?"

"Yes. But with the weather and the mountains, I couldn't get a decent signal. I looked at Rick and asked him if he was okay. He looked pale. I was afraid then that he'd been seriously injured."

He stared, each word she spoke piercing him like a hot

poker. They hurt more than the day *he'd* been shot at. The day his Kevlar vest saved his life. The impact of the bullet had left one hell of a bruise on his chest, but he'd survived. "Had you or Rick been hit, yet?"

Her hand splayed out across her belly. "I looked over at Rick and asked him again. But he shook his head." She seemed to want to add more.

"I tried to call again, and I got someone. I don't remember who it was. I called for the QRF."

"The QRF?"

"Quick Reaction Force. A platoon of infantry trained to respond immediately to any situation. Whoever I was talking to asked where I was. I didn't know exactly where we were."

"You don't have GPS on your truck?"

She shook her head. "No. It was just a cargo truck. Only the armored vehicles have GPS. I gave him a ballpark grid reference and he asked what the hell was I doing way out there."

"Grid reference?"

She nodded. "It's a method of locating points on a map."

The air hung heavy around them. The way she'd paused, the wary look that had seeped into her eyes, all his intuition grabbed him hard. "Go on."

Her voice dropped. "I told him, and he said that, according to a memo he'd just got, the outpost had been abandoned the week before. The Germans had moved to another location. I had the wrong grid reference.

"I've had a lot of time to think about this and I know what happened. The outpost had been abandoned, yes, but someone in the German contingent wanted us to go up there to be ambushed. That was why they asked for a whole pile of stuff, like ammo, radios and batteries.

And fuel.'' She stared at him, her eyes wide and yet, angry. ''Basically, there had been a major security breach.''

He was stunned. ''And that's why you were made to sign that nondisclosure agreement?''

''We all sign it when we retire. But yes, that's why Major Tirouski insisted I keep quiet. They had a big problem on their hands and if the media got hold of security breach, you-know-what would hit the fan.''

He frowned at her, the hairs on his arms rising. ''Did Tirouski ever talk to you?''

She swallowed. ''He came here one day shortly after you arrived. He wanted to make sure I was keeping my mouth shut.''

''A long trip for just that.''

She looked away and shrugged. ''This was a big problem, and he was on government time.''

Something wasn't right, and again the old suspicions reared. Somehow he forced himself to bide his time. ''Did you make it into the back of the truck? Did Rick get shot then?''

Sylvie looked up at him, almost as if she'd been lost in her thoughts. ''We did manage to get into the truck, but no, Rick had already been shot. I think he'd been hit right when they opened fire on us. But it was too dark for me to notice any blood.''

Her words were all jumbling about in his mind. He shook his head. ''Did Rick know he'd been shot?''

She nodded.

It wasn't making sense. ''Why did he lie?''

She shrugged. ''I don't know. Denial, not wanting to be a burden to me. Scared.'' She met his gaze with caution. ''Rick was really scared. We both were, yes, who wouldn't be, but Rick was terrified.''

Jon didn't know what to say. He tried to swallow, but his mouth was dry.

"Rick was a good soldier," she rushed out. "It was okay to be scared. Don't compare him to yourself when you're in the line of fire, or even me. Rick was young, and didn't have the experience I had. He hadn't been hardened like the older, more seasoned soldiers. He couldn't put his emotions aside and focus on what had to be done."

He gaped at her. What was she saying?

She continued. "When we got into the back of the truck, I saw that he was injured. I tried the cell phone again, to let them know we had an injury. But it didn't work inside the box. Too much steel plating, I guess. If only Rick had told me earlier that he was injured."

Jon blinked. That explained the anger at the two-way radio. She hadn't been able to report that Rick was hurt. "It's all right. I understand. Rick wouldn't have wanted anyone to think he couldn't do his job. He'd been shot in the leg, and must have thought that it wasn't as bad as it was. After all, the injury killed him."

Sylvie paled. "Yes, he was conscientious," she murmured.

Jon pulled her close. "I don't need to know any more."

She pushed out of his embrace. Still ashen, she took another step back. "Yes, you do. That's only what happened outside of the truck."

He shook his head. "What did you do inside of the truck?"

She straightened her shoulders, her expression now tight and distraught. "I killed Rick."

Chapter 15

What? Did he hear her right?

Frowning, he tried to ask her to repeat herself, but he couldn't. Somehow the air in his lungs refused to move through his vocal cords.

What had she just said?

She backed away. He searched her face, but she wouldn't meet his eyes.

Finally he blurted out, "What did you say?"

She bit her lip, her hands wringing over and over until he wanted to grab them and force them down to her sides.

"Answer me!"

She jumped. "I killed him! Or as good as. Please, Jon, don't say anything until I tell you the whole story. Please?"

He did nothing, and the long seconds ticked into minutes. Finally he nodded, a slow, wooden movement.

Her voice quavered. "After we got into the truck, I put the combat lock on. That's the lock on the inside. It was pitch-black, but I managed to find the dome light. That's when I saw he was injured." She seemed to steel herself for a proper explanation. "You see, Rick tried to stand, but he slumped down and I grabbed him. Only then did I see he'd been injured. I asked him where, and he said his leg.

"We didn't have a first-aid kit back there, so I tore off Rick's field-dressing kit. He had taped it to his webbing here." She touched her right shoulder. "I gave him first aid. He hadn't been bleeding a lot, but I managed to bandage it. He said his leg was going numb. That's when I tried to call again, but I had lost the signal.

"I wanted to go back outside, to call the camp. I can remember that now, but…" With her fingers she pressed her eyebrows together and shook her head. "It was unsafe. Rick couldn't cover me properly. Then…then the dome light went out. At the time we didn't know if those who shot at us had cut the battery cable or the battery had just died. It went out quickly, I remember, and Rick swore. By then, he was pretty scared. The wind picked up and we could feel the truck wobble. Those trucks have a very high center of gravity, and they get buffeted about in a strong breeze. I decided it was too dangerous for me to go outside alone."

She paused, inhaling and exhaling several times as if to stop herself from shaking. "We expected to be blown up at any minute. I kept wondering if hiding in the truck had been the best thing to do. But there was no other place to go. We'd entered a long, narrow gorge, where the road was only one lane wide. And we had no idea where the weapons fire had come from. I couldn't go out again. I pulled off Rick's flashlight. He had his attached to his webbing at the left shoulder. Mine was gone. It must have come off when we were crawling under the truck. I hung his flashlight up and lit it and we sat and waited.''

She stared at the floor. "You have no idea how much I regret what I did after that. All I could think about was the way I'd lived my life. Or *not* lived it."

She shut her eyes, her expression pinched and pained. He had no idea what she meant by that last statement. His insides clenched, and he wanted to scream. How he held it in, he couldn't guess. His jaw tight, he asked, "How did you kill him, Sylvie? How?"

She looked up at his dark features. "Think about how far along I am. When you met me, I was twelve weeks along." She paused. "You do the math."

He counted backward, struggling to focus on the simple math. Oh, damn. Holy cow. "Are you telling me you got pregnant that night?"

She nodded, briefly. "I can't believe it hadn't occurred to you before."

"I…I just assumed you and Rick had been having sex regularly." Damn, it hurt to say that. She and Rick. He'd always assumed they'd been lovers. *In love.* And that assumption had kept him from exploring the attraction that he felt for Sylvie.

Until last night, when it hadn't matter one damn iota.

Her laugh was short and hollow. "No. Rick and I had been friends only. Nothing more. Until that night." She mouthed a mild curse, and he knew she was slipping into the past.

"Rick needed more than comfort." Her words came out in short, rushed blocks, as if she could barely say them. "He asked to make love to me. He said he'd always cared for me. It was as if he knew he was going to die."

She stopped, and Jon vaguely noticed her struggle to

contain her grief. "I didn't want to. I'd always made it a personal policy not to get involved with any soldier. I wasn't the only woman who thought like that. A lot of female soldiers had the same idea. We'd seen men at their worst, and believe me, it's not pretty, especially the young guys."

"But you did...."

She jerked her head up and down swiftly. She was about to speak when she paused and peered at him with confusion in her eyes. "You haven't figured it out yet, have you?"

He blinked and shook his head.

"I was a virgin, and when Rick began to fall apart on me, and I knew he believed he was going to die, I started to think about it as well." She wet her lips. "I realized I didn't want to die a virgin. I had no life outside of the military, and suddenly it occurred to me that I was going to die without ever experiencing...sex. So I agreed when he suggested it."

The air escaped from him, hard and fast as if he'd been sucker punched. He tilted his head in disbelief. "You had sex with him? How could he even, I mean, he was injured!"

"There wasn't that much blood loss. He seemed to have come around, and he needed me—"

"He needed someone with some common sense!"

"He seemed fine. He was scared!"

"Fine? Damn, woman, he was dying! All you could think about was having a good time?"

She flew at him, quickly enough to make him blink and step back. "I was selfish, all right! I admit it! But for a while, it kept Rick going, and even I needed some comfort. We both could have died out there." Her voice dropped. "I would have thought that you'd figured it all out."

He shut his mouth to the angry volley he was ready to fling. All those clues, evidence that he'd ignored. She'd turned him on so much, just being Sylvie, that he didn't consider her lack of experience making love. But each odd move, each kiss that had more enthusiasm than expertise, all those looks that he knew were virginal and innocent. God, she was a hell of a lot more innocent than he'd figured.

He glared at her. "And you're telling me that he got you pregnant that one time?"

She nodded. "I was more concerned with the possibility of dying a virgin than with doing my job." She met his glare with equal intensity. "The only time I get involved with another soldier, I get pregnant. One time— because I was too scared to do my job! You can't even begin to understand how that makes me feel. Rick died because I let my emotions get the better of me! But Rick needed to take his mind off his injury."

Jon slapped the wall beside him. "He was dying! You wasted his energy on sex, when he should have been fighting for his life?"

She leaned toward him, her own voice rising until it cracked. "I made a mistake! Like last night, when I was so desperate to be someone else because I…I can't stand who I really am! Besides, you didn't mind wasting your energy!"

"I wasn't bleeding to death!"

She pursed her lips.

He couldn't believe what was happening. What *had* happened. Sylvie seemed on the edge of losing control, and even though a part of him recognized her anguish—

hell—even wanted to pull her into his arms to stop it, a bigger, more painful part stopped him.

But she carried his only living relative. He should have some compassion.

No.

"You killed him after that?" His lungs burned from lack of air, and he fought back the swirls of anger, hurt and bitterness. He shouldn't be here, interrogating her. He should call Major Tirouski and tell him everything, demand a full investigation and the full truth.

And let Sylvie take her punishment like the damned good soldier she was supposed to be.

"Rick fell unconscious as soon as we finished. I tried to wake him up but couldn't." She looked heavenward, blinking rapidly, clenching her teeth. "I'll always wonder at the irony. He died in a way every man wants to go. But I know that doesn't make it right."

She dropped her gaze to his. Still defiant, still the Sylvie he had damnably fallen head-over-heels in love with. "I know I should have been braver, tightened the bandages, stopped his suggestion and told him it was just his fear talking. Or maybe I should have raced outside and emptied both weapons into the entire gorge! All over the place, because we didn't even know where the shots came from!" She pounded her chest. "I know I should have tried harder to keep him alive! I have to live with that! I was a coward that night."

She spun around, her mouth set hard. "I know I killed him, as much as that bastard who pulled the trigger." She shot Jon a desperate look over her shoulder. "I know it doesn't change anything, but I...I..."

She looked hollow, tortured, and one desperate heart-beat later, he ached to shut out all his fury and just hold her.

Forgive her.

But…he couldn't.

She finally finished her sentence. ''…I'm sorry.''

He couldn't think. He couldn't say anything. Stunned, he stood there until the first idea pricked at his numb body.

He snatched up all his papers, crushing some with such force that the sharp corners of the unopened autopsy envelope dug into his callused palms.

Then, without another word, he flung one scathing glare at Sylvie, ground his heel into the living room carpet and spun away. He stalked out to the kitchen, the back door, the bunkhouse.

And eventually all the way to his home in Toronto.

Chapter 16

The day wasn't the sort of day Jon could associate with cemeteries. Clear and sunny, warmer than the first part of November should have been, and no hint at all of the bad weather coming.

He pushed forward, ignoring the gardener who drove a small leaf vacuum in neat, even strips. The large oak tree to his left had been the last to shed its coppery leaves.

The graves he wanted were at the far end. But even at this distance he could spy a figure crouching down in front of them.

The swell of indignation died when the figure stood. It was Carter Rosenberg, his father's old partner and best friend, the man in whose arms his father had died. Jon had been at his retirement party a few months back.

Carter turned when he heard Jon approach. His gaze held no surprise. He'd been expecting Jon.

"Hello." The older man glanced up at the clear sky

with heavy, well-lined features. "Nice day to be outside."

Jon stared at him, then finally nodded. Both men turned their attention to the three graves. Jon's mother and father, their stones wide and tastefully decorated by the gardener. Jon had paid for the service years ago.

And Rick's. He swallowed as he read again the simple military stone memorial. Below the cross was etched Rick's name and rank and corps. Below that, his life span. So damn short.

"I remember when he was born," Carter murmured.

"So do I."

Carter looked at him. "He was a good kid. Died in the service of peace. Like your father, Jon. Your dad would be proud. And I heard his name has been added to the Book of Remembrance."

Jon clenched his jaw. That book was a great honor, but today it didn't feel like it. "He was just a kid."

"Old enough, I hear."

He shot the old man a wary look. "Old enough to serve his country?"

Carter twisted around, his expression unyieldingly tough. Uncharacteristically tough. "Old enough to father a child, I mean."

"Where'd you hear that?"

"Word gets around, Jon." He folded his arms. "And he was old enough to know that with life comes death. And the living have to move on."

"I have, Carter."

"Drove past your house again yesterday. Garbage day."

"So?"

"I've been driving a lot, lately. The wife likes to go out for coffee with me. Says she missed all those times

I spent in coffee shops with your father, and wants to make up for it.''

What the hell was he getting at?

"Jon, we drive by your house every garbage day."

"Thinking of a second career?"

Carter laughed. "Nope. But I did notice how little garbage you have."

"I live alone."

"Yes, you do. Did your brother have much stuff, Jon?"

He stiffened. "Not much."

"Not like Tanya, when she left. You threw out a bunch of stuff then, didn't you?"

"She didn't need it anymore, and neither did I."

Carter watched him, that impenetrable look setting up shop on his face. "You haven't been through Rick's stuff yet, have you?"

Jon felt the burn of heat seep into his face. "That's none of your concern."

Carter unfolded his arms. He gestured with his head for them to move back toward the road. Jon gave one last look to Rick's grave before following the older man. He'd be back before the snow came. There was still time.

They walked in silence for a few minutes.

"Saw Tanya the other day," Carter said. "She asked about you."

Jon said nothing.

"She's gone on with her life, Jon."

"So have I."

Carter stopped and grabbed his arm. "No, you haven't, son. When your father died and later, when his murderer walked out of that courtroom a free man, you faced the fact that your father wasn't coming back. You moved on with your life then. Were you ever mad at me?"

Shocked, Jon gaped at him. "Never! You were just doing your job."

"The woman Rick was with when he died was just doing her job, too."

He gritted his teeth. "No, she wasn't. And she even admitted as much."

"I wasn't there and neither were you, so you can't say for sure. Jon, you've stared at the wrong end of a gun a time or two. It gets a person thinking differently. Like when a woman betrays a man."

Jon started walking again. "What the hell are you talking about?"

"You never fully dealt with Tanya's departure, Jon," Carter called out.

He didn't look back. "I did. I threw out her junk and went back to work."

"All you did was clean out your house. Which is a hell of a lot more than you did with Rick."

Jon stopped, spun around and stalked back to the old man. The wind picked up a thin wisp of white hair from the top of the man's head. Before Jon could speak, Carter continued, "You didn't grieve her. I didn't say anything because it comes in everyone's own time. But it's time to grieve both Tanya *and* Rick. Especially Rick. He deserves it."

"I did grieve him."

Carter sighed. "It's easy to fool yourself when there's no one around to challenge you, isn't it? That's why you're always alone." His expression softened. "But it's time to challenge that stupid notion. You worked hard after your father died because you could battle the crime that killed him. But you couldn't fight the thing that caused Tanya to leave you, and you most certainly couldn't fight the crime that killed Rick."

"What killed Rick is out in Alberta, pregnant with his baby!"

Finally, Carter showed surprise. Feeling a bit smug, Jon plowed on, "That's right. She admitted she'd as good as killed him."

"She told you?"

"That's right."

"Brave woman."

"No, she's not."

"Yes, she is. But you're mad because she lived and Rick didn't."

Jon stopped his retort. Yeah, all right, Sylvie was brave, and yeah, he was mad. Still. But she'd lied to him, and kept secrets from him, and because of her his brother was dead. He glared at Carter, squinting against the brilliant sun. "All right, she is, but I'm still thinking of turning her into the military so she can get her punishment."

Carter lifted his eyebrows. "What's taking you so long?"

Jon jerked back.

Patiently Carter waited for the answer they both knew he couldn't give. Finally the older man tilted his head. "How do you know for sure that woman was responsible for Rick's death? What did the autopsy report say? You're a police officer, you should be checking the evidence first before you go off half-cocked."

Jon turned and resumed his swift pace back to his car, the heat of another embarrassing question flooding into him.

"You haven't read it yet, have you, Jon?" Carter called out. "It's time to. You're brave enough to be a cop in this city. It's time to be brave enough to bury your brother."

Jon kept walking straight to his car. He had planned

to go to the Yonge Street Mission to meet a pastor there for talk of expanding the small bike club he'd created for the kids, but instead he drove straight home.

His living room looked exactly as it had for the past six months. He'd shoved Rick's effects to one corner, and since coming home from Alberta, he'd taken to watching TV in his bedroom.

On top of the barrack boxes was the final report. He'd never even finished reading it, for Pete's sake. Carter was so right. He hadn't got as far as the complete autopsy report.

With a deep breath he picked it up and pulled it out of the envelope.

The autopsy report shook as he read it. Its final assessment glared up at him and he folded it up and put it away again.

Sylvie's words slipped free of his memory and he pondered them. The military had given her the wrong directions to the outpost. What had she called those directions? Grid reference? There had been a major security problem and that was why they'd wanted the whole incident hushed up and why Tirouski had visited the ranch to ensure Sylvie did her part. And she'd had her own personal reasons to agree.

But Sylvie hadn't precipitated Rick's death. He'd died from an embolic stroke, caused "probably from injury to the femoral artery," the medical examiner had written.

The paper below swam in his vision. He slapped it on the coffee table and slid to the floor, reaching for a barrack box.

Chapter 17

The kitchen calendar glared at Sylvie that morning. Just as it had glared at her every other morning since Jon had left.

He'd been gone for four months. One hundred and twenty days. Sylvie ripped her gaze from the offending calendar and while rubbing her aching, itchy belly, she threw open the refrigerator. She should be counting the days till the baby's arrival, and not the ones since the baby's uncle left.

She slammed the refrigerator door shut. Supper would be light and only for her, so there was no need to start preparing it this early in the morning. Lawrence, Purley and Dad were to take the steers into Calgary. Andrea had gone to visit her sister in Vancouver. Michael had finally had his shoulder operated on, and was down in Fort MacLeod staying with his mother while he recuperated.

Sylvie was alone.

The growl of an engine outside intensified and then immediately stopped.

She peered out the window in time to catch her father climbing out of the big truck they'd rented. Behind him, steam rose from the long, slatted cattle trailer. They were ready to leave.

Her father threw open the back door. "We're off. Are you going to be all right? You still look tired."

She forced a smile on her face. "I *am* tired. The baby did another bout of gymnastics last night and I'm the one with the sore muscles."

Allister smiled back. "Well, he'll stop soon. He's getting too big. Oh, while you were in the shower, the rental store called. We must have left one of the spare hooks for the come-along in the line shack last summer, and they've just missed it. Can you call them to say we'll look for it later this week?"

"Sure." She couldn't find the energy to remove her smile.

Still at the door, her father studied her. "Hey, bud, chin up. Give him time."

She lifted her brows. He hadn't called her bud for years.

He didn't understand her, not completely. He thought that she was mooning over Jon. She wasn't. She couldn't afford the time. No, Jon had left. She'd given him what he wanted, the truth about Rick's death. Too bad it wouldn't help him find closure. It hadn't helped her find any.

One thing did puzzle her. She'd been waiting for the ax to fall from the military, but it hadn't. Jon must not have taken his accusations back to Major Tirouski.

She thrust aside the pain that ached in her belly and

concentrated on her father. "It's been over four months. He's gone, Dad. He wasn't the kind to stick around."

"Maybe so, but listen, bud. You did what you thought was right. It wasn't your fault that that young fellow died. And there isn't anything you can do about it now." Allister's mouth thinned as he paused. "If Andrea calls, tell her I'll call her when I get to the hotel." He winked at her, but his face stayed grim. "I'll see you in a couple of days, okay, bud?"

"Sure."

Then she was alone again.

In the living room, she put on a brave face for the wave goodbye. After they disappeared down the drive, she glanced around.

Suddenly the day stretched ahead like a colossal set of steep stairs. She still had over a month to carry her baby, and climbing even the few steps into the house felt like a chore some days. Today was going to be one of those days.

Sylvie made a token effort to straighten the magazines on the coffee table, but ended up dropping them. No nesting instinct today.

Leaving the housework, she grabbed the pickup's keys and her jacket and headed outside. Crisp air greeted her, and she inhaled deeply. The day smelled of snow. Already the sun had relinquished its strength to the line of gray clouds sliding over the mountains.

She'd go to the line shack, find the hook and return it. A trip into town would do her good. The last time she'd bothered to go in was to mail Jon's paycheck, in care of the Toronto Police Services. The following month's bank statement confirmed that he'd cashed it.

In the privacy of her office, she'd run her finger over the canceled check, over his strong, scrawling signature, finding a hollow comfort in knowing he'd touched it, until the embarrassment of the act forced her to tuck the check into the bank file.

Pulling up on her jacket's collar, she shook off the ridiculous, depressing thoughts. Only positive thoughts, she reminded herself. The counselor from Veterans Affairs had experience with PTSD. She'd given Sylvie sound advice, exercises, even a shoulder to cry on. And time. Lots of time to accept her mistakes and the fear she'd faced and learn to wait until the baby was born before she could take medication. The counselor had told Sylvie to live for the future.

Without Jon?

Sylvie hauled herself heavily into the pickup. One day at a time, and today's duty was to find that hook.

An hour later she spotted the line shack. Her idea of straightening the wall had worked beautifully. That day Lawrence had nodded with satisfaction, and for the first time since Jon's departure, she'd smiled with genuine pleasure.

Pulling up in front, Sylvie grimaced suddenly. The baby had decided to stretch. *Again.* Twinges and that constant tight heaviness had made the bouncing trip out here even more uncomfortable. Oh, but she would be glad to get this pregnancy over and done with. She was big, even the doctor had said so at her last checkup.

With a groan, she heaved herself out of the truck. The line shack stood straight and tall. Purley had even given it a fresh coat of light-blue paint.

Several bold flakes of snow pranced down in front of her. Beyond, a line of white dusted the rising hills. She'd been right about the smell of snow.

She hurried into the shack.

Inside she waited for her eyes to adjust to the dimness.

A simple bench lined the left side and an old woodstove jutted out on the other, beside a small cupboard. Some scraps of wood discarded after they'd repaired the hut were stacked neatly on the other side of the stove, waiting to be burned.

Years ago Lawrence had brought out the beaten-up cupboard and in it, he'd shoved a pot, a bottle of water—now frozen—and some candles and matches.

And there, in the corner, lay the hook.

She walked over and bent down.

A pain ripped through her, buckling her knees and scraping the breath from her lungs.

Gasping for breath, she splayed out her mittened hands and dropped to the floor. *Oh, damn, another pulled muscle?* She really didn't need this. Waiting a moment, on all fours, she practiced her breathing. In and count, two…three…four…five and out two…three…four…five.

The pain subsided. Grabbing the cold stove, she strained to pull herself to standing. Well, no trip to town today. She needed a little rest—

The spasm hit again with equal vigor. She swore and bit her lip.

Another followed, stretching itself mercilessly around her wide belly to her back.

She had to get home. And lie down. A cold pack on her belly. *Yes.* Something soothing.

Clutching the hook, she staggered to the door. She gripped the old-fashioned handle as yet another spasm struck, this one twisting her muscles until she grimaced and groaned.

Don't be such a wimp, she ordered herself. If you can't handle a pulled muscle, you'll never handle labor.

She threw open the door.

Snow whipped in around her in a single, frenzied swirl.
Snow so heavy she could barely make out the dark form
of the truck. Already a thick layer of white buried the
dry, crusty ground.

She wanted to curse, but another contraction wrenched
through her, stretching out in a nauseating wave until it
cruised over her hips and clawed into her lower back.

The baby protested the cramp and kicked hard.

And water gushed down her inner thighs.

Oh, God, was her water supposed to fill her boots? She
stood, shocked into stillness, feeling the warmth stream
down her legs. Another spasm tore at her and she had to
hold tight to the door handle to keep herself upright.

Oh no. Oh please, no, not now!

Please, let me please just be peeing myself.

The water poured on, until she slammed shut the door
and somehow made it to the bench.

She collapsed onto her side on the hard wood and shut
her eyes to the tears that threatened.

Water seeped out, through her pants. A steady drip-
drip cut through the sounds of the rising wind outside.

She couldn't deny what was happening.

She was in labor. Nearly six weeks too soon.

Lord, please keep my baby safe. Please.

The pain eased and she took advantage of the relative
comfort to relax. Deep breaths. In and out. Easy. Like
they'd taught her. Exhalations as long as the inhalations.
Easy does it.

She lingered a few quiet minutes until she felt she
could sit up. Gingerly, she pushed herself from the rough,
cold pine, up to the sitting position. She had to get home.
She *could* get home. It would be a bumpy, wet, sloshy
ride, and she'd have to empty her boots first, but she

could do it. She had enough time. The nurse at the prenatal classes said most first-time mothers had tons of
time. Babies weren't born instantly, certainly not according to the stories she'd heard from the other mothers at
the classes.

Gripping the edge of the seat, she pushed herself to
standing. There, she could do it. Now to make it to the
truck.

She threw open the door again, wincing at the glare of
total white. A snow squall. Another Alberta clipper.

Oh, Lord, please stop it. Make it go away.

Icy snow sprayed her face as another contraction grew
deep in her, frighteningly different in feeling.

With slow, deliberate tightening, the new contraction
hardened in her below her navel and swept its painful
way around to settle like a hot lava rock in her back. The
same way the other contractions felt, but this one was
very, very different.

Strengthening, hardening, focused in power and purpose, the pain peaked, stretched out again around her and
held her for torturing ransom. Labor was supposed to be
hard, painful, but this hard? This painful?

As she clung to the door to wait it out, she knew the
horrible truth.

She'd never make it across the rolling pastureland to
the house in a snow squall, with hard labor starting six
weeks early and coming with an intensity that had forced
her to her wet and watery knees, blurred her vision and
left her gasping for a pain-free breath.

Oh no. She was going to have her baby.

Here, now, in this line shack.

As alone as she'd always been, as she'd always hated
to be. Alone and as scared as she'd been months ago,

shivering with fear in that supply truck, beside Rick who'd fallen unconscious and would never wake up.

Tears streamed down her face, freezing as a blast of the uncaring wind hit her square on.

God would take her little baby's life. And maybe hers, too.

Poetic justice for killing the father.

Chapter 18

Where the heck was she?

Jon pivoted around the wide kitchen and back into the hall. He headed straight for Sylvie's bedroom. Touching the slightly ajar door, he called out, "Sylvie?"

On silent hinges the door swung open, revealing rumpled bedclothes, a laundry basket of neatly folded baby clothes, a book, opened and upside down on the bedside table, *Dealing with Life's Major Changes.*

He returned to the kitchen, noting that only half of the dishes were dried, the tea towel spread across those that remained in the rack. He pushed through to the back door. Someone had to be around. In the bunkhouse, maybe? The barn, feeding that demanding pig?

The truck was gone. Sylvie's little car still remained, but the long cattle trailer was also gone. Lawrence had told him they owned the trailer, but every fall, rented a larger truck to pull it.

Damn. Had she decided to go with them when they took the steers to market?

Someone should know.

The bunkhouse was empty, as was the campground office. Bruce greeted him at the barn, snorting and snuffling around his feet. Suspicious geese peered at him from behind their pen, telling him nothing.

The whole damn place was deserted.

She couldn't have gone with the whole crew to Calgary for the cattle auction. They'd need a bus to carry everyone. If she'd gone to town, he'd have seen her. He'd driven past the feed store, the grocery store and the doctor's office. He'd have seen the pickup.

Where the hell was she?

Returning to the kitchen, the only place that had shown any life at all today, Jon tapped impatient fingers on the counter.

The ranch owned a cell phone. Someone would have it on. He'd caught the unpleasant forecast. Light snow, colder temps and squalls coming down from in the mountains. If they'd taken the steers to Calgary, they'd have their cell phone on, especially on a day like today. The snow had already started here, the mountains beyond the ranch now obscured by one mother of a squall.

The number? What the hell was the number? Remembering where Sylvie had scrawled it for him, he strode to the calendar and ripped it off the wall. There, on June's page, he found it.

Abruptly the memory of when Sylvie had scrawled out the number returned, sharp and pungent. She'd written it there for his benefit.

Thank you, Sylvie.

He quickly dialed the number, tapping his foot as he urged someone to answer it.

"Hello?"

"Lawrence, is that you?"

"Yep." A pause. "Jon?"

"Yeah, it's me."

"The number on the phone here says you're at the house. What the heck are you doing there?"

Jon drew in a breath. "Never mind that, look is—"

Lawrence's voice still held surprise as he interrupted him. "We didn't think we'd ever see you again. What's brought you back, son?"

He gritted his teeth. He'd acted like an ass this summer, walking out on all of them, without so much as a goodbye. Had Sylvie explained to the others why he'd left?

"Look, now isn't the time to go into all that," he answered. "Is Sylvie with you?"

"No! She's not at home? Wonder where she is."

A lump grew in his chest. "Where are you?"

"We're halfway to Calgary. Sylvie can't be far. Did you check the barn?"

"The whole place is deserted."

Lawrence made thoughtful noise. "Well, hang tough, son. She'll show up."

Jon rang off. He didn't have much of a choice but to wait, did he? Wherever Sylvie was, she'd have to come home sooner or later.

And he'd be there. He had a lot to say to her.

Trouble was, something—he wasn't sure what—didn't feel right.

The baby was coming. At least she'd meet the little guy before they both died.

At the sound of one wild gust as it rattled the shack, she twisted around to face the window. The squall had intensified, the accompanying drafts finding their way through small cracks missed when they'd installed a few bags of insulation and vapor barrier. One strong draft chilled her face.

She was truly alone. Suddenly the fear she'd felt in the truck in Bosnia, watching Rick die, paled. And it wasn't a slight on Rick. God, his death had been so unfair. No, this concerned his baby, a child whose birth would be witnessed by the same specter of death.

Tears burned like acid in her eyes. She didn't want this baby to end its life before it had even started. No.

No! Oh, God, she could hardly breathe!

And Jon would never meet his brother's baby.

The thought of Jon losing another relative hurt the most, more than the next contraction that grew with barbaric strength inside her.

She breathed through the pain, in and counting, out and counting, tears of dread welling in her eyes. Jon didn't deserve this lot in life. She might never see him again, but he deserved his little nephew or niece.

And he *would* see the poor little baby.

As the next contraction subsided, she struggled to her feet and stumbled over to the woodstove. Everything was there to make a fire. She'd get this line shack warm and bring Jon's only living relative into the world and do her best to save its life. He deserved that much.

As the newspaper caught and licked comforting flames around the kindling, a clear understanding glowed through her. In the long stretch of time since Jon had left, she'd relived and what-if'd the night Rick died to the point of exasperation.

Yes, she'd been a coward. She'd made a mistake, but so had the military. But they'd corrected the fault and moved on.

And though Jon may always blame her, she had tried to keep his brother alive as well as she could have.

Now it was time to move on herself and do something good for a change.

Like save her baby's life.

She found the frozen bottle of water and set it close to the fire. Once it thawed, she'd boil it and wash up as best she could. She wasn't going to take the coward's way out this time, even if it killed her.

The phone rang. Jon shoved aside the chair and leaped for the receiver. "Sylvie?"

"No. It's me, Allister."

Jon sagged.

"Look, Jon, Lawrence tells me Sylvie's not there. She back yet?"

"No."

"Is her car there?"

"Yes, but the truck is gone. And I didn't see it in town, either."

"How long have you been there?"

"Over an hour."

Allister swore. "Look, I told her the rental place in town called to say we'd left a hook for the come-along out in the line shack. I told her to call them to say either Lawrence or I would get it when we returned."

A short stream of words far worse than Allister's curse spewed from his mouth. "She's gone out there, damn it!" He glared out the window, his frown fading as he watched the weather worsen.

Something was wrong. Never had the intuitive warning hit him so hard, even counting the time Rick's CO had hung up on him and left Jon with a knot of suspicion in his gut the size of a football.

He gripped the receiver, his whitened knuckles aching as he stared out the window. "I gotta get out to the line shack. I can see a squall coming down from the mountains. Look, Allister, call back here every five minutes. If Sylvie answers, tell her to stay put." He slammed the phone down and raced outside.

The icy wind sucked his breath away, but he barreled into his rental car. He knew the chances of getting stuck were dangerously high with such a low-riding vehicle, but searching out the ATV would take too blasted long.

He gunned the engine and sailed through the open gates to the pasture. Not hard to remember the way to the line shack when every night you dream of the trip back on horseback, with Sylvie. With his arms around Sylvie and the rear edge of the saddle nearly slicing through his erection.

Come on. *Come on!* He spun out in one spot several kilometers from the house, but managed to straighten before he became disoriented. The tires bit into the snow and frozen scrubgrass, broadcasting icy dirt everywhere. He glanced at the speedometer. Sixty kilometers an hour. He'd been driving for ten minutes. Damn, he should be able to see the line shack by now.

Mother, if he'd been off even a degree or two back there when he'd entered the paddock, he'd be miles away from the shack by now. Squinting through the driving snow, he searched the horizon. At one short point in time, the sun broke through the squall. Mountains gleamed white blue behind the roll of foothills.

There it was! He swerved hard, dipping into a low stretch once used as a watering hole. The car protested, and for a heartbeat, Jon was sure he'd roll the vehicle like a toy.

Downshifting, he slammed hard on the accelerator, and

the car spun its way up the other side, its front bumper cutting into the hard ground. The line shack loomed momentarily in another clear break.

Yes! The truck was parked askew in front, but—his heart leaped to his throat—the driver door stood open. And, he blinked, snow had already drifted in onto the seat.

How long had it been there? Where was Sylvie?

Another squall swallowed up the truck again.

Something had gone wrong. *Something was really, really wrong.*

Soaring over the far edge, Jon braced himself for the impact of his low-riding sports car hitting the hard ground.

It wasn't any less than he expected. He slammed into the steering wheel. Damn, he'd forgotten to buckle his seat belt. Gearing up, he pushed the engine harder through the swirling snow.

The truck appeared abruptly, way too close. Too late, Jon rammed his foot on the brakes. "Holy f—"

He was going to broadside Sylvie's truck.

At sixty kilometers per hour.

Chapter 19

Groggily Jon sat up, tasting blood in his mouth from where he'd slammed into the steering wheel.

He blinked away the brain fog, squinted away the memory of the crushing metal and breaking glass that still rang in his head.

Sylvie!

Scrambling out of the car, he screamed out her name. He tore around the truck and slipped once, nearly losing his footing as he struggled to reach the door.

He threw it open.

"Sylvie!"

She lay on the bench, her eyes shut, her jacket shed and wrapped around her abdomen. Beside her was the come-along hook. The air was still, a scent he couldn't recognize lingering over the fading odor of burning wood.

Inside the door was a pool of water, now crusting over

with ice. He ground the tiny shards underfoot as he stalked over to her.

"Sylvie!"

Her eyelids pressed tightly shut, as her brows knitted together. She drew a deep hiss in between clenched teeth. In the dim light, he could see her face redden.

"Jon?"

He grabbed her hand. "It's me. Open your eyes. Tell me what's happening."

She opened her eyes and glared at him as she bit down on the words, "I'm having the freaking baby!"

Jon froze, a curse caught in his throat as shock chilled his muscles.

He threw off the fear as he scanned the shack. "We've got to get you out of here." He did a quick survey. She didn't seem hurt, but her pants were soaking. Her water had broken. "Sylvie, you've got to sit up. Remember what the nurse said? You shouldn't lie down. It cuts off the blood flow."

She nodded, gripping his arm as he helped her sit up. Once she'd stopped weaving, he turned around and grabbed a large log. He shoved in behind her and covered it with his coat. She eased out of the way, so he could use the bottom hem to pad her buttocks.

Knees fallen open, she sat forward, humped over her swollen belly. She'd grown big since he left.

Oh, boy. He had to get her out of here.

In what?

With a glance to the door, he did a quick mental calculation. He'd investigated enough traffic accidents to know that slamming into her truck with his car had made both vehicles useless.

Dread washed over him.

He leaned behind the startled Sylvie and grabbed his

cell phone from his coat pocket. "Honey, I'll have to call 911."

She flung her head back and pressed her hands on her abdomen. "Gee, Sherlock, you went to the police academy for that? Argg!"

The cell phone slipped from his hands and dropped to the floor. Cursing, he picked it up. "I'm afraid I just smashed both of our vehicles up. I have to call for help, okay?"

"Don't bother with 911, Jon," she gritted out. "The ambulance in town won't make it here and they wouldn't know where to go, anyway."

"Let them make that decision, okay?"

She grabbed his hand, her fingers digging into the tendons at his wrist. "They won't get here in time!"

Jon stared at her. Was she right? How the hell were they going to get help, then? Damn, he wished he'd listened more carefully to Lawrence's long lessons on childbirth. Instead, he'd been wrapped up in searching for answers—answers that didn't matter one blasted iota anymore.

"Wait!" He straightened the phone and dialed a number, praying he had it right after all these months.

Sylvie looked up. "Who are you calling?"

"Major Tirouski."

"Are you nuts? What's he going to do? Look, Jon, we're having this baby here. I don't want—"

"Major?" He hated to cut her off midsentence, but damn it, the major was their only hope.

A few minutes later, after he'd turned away from Sylvie, he hung up.

She shifted to get more comfortable. "What did he say?"

Jon sat beside her, taking her hand and brushing the

strand of wayward hair from her eyes. "He said he's sending the local militia's doctor out in the 'box-amb.' Whatever that is."

Sylvie nodded. "It's a four-wheel-drive ambulance. Actually, I think it'll work. The driver should know where we are. They come out here and cross our land all summer long." She was breathing heavily.

He brushed her face with his hand. "Hang in there, hon. They'll be here soon."

She shook her head. She tried to laugh, but it came out in a heavy, short burst. "They won't make it in time, Jon." Another contraction hit. "Ohh! Talk to me. Take my mind off these contractions, *please*."

He stood. "I will, hon. First up, I'll fix that fire. Then we have to get you ready." Holy mother, how could he sound so calm?

"Jon!"

He turned. She was rocking herself, her face blotchy and pinched.

"Why are you here?"

He stopped crumpling the newspaper. "Because I love you. I was hurt by what you'd told me about Rick, and I had to leave right away before I did something really stupid." He checked his panic. He was a cop. He could handle the tough stuff. "But…lately I've come to see that you were coping the only way you knew how, both in the truck that night and, you know, this past summer. You'd been traumatized and well…you managed. He scrunched up the paper again. "Look, I'd lost a brother, but you believed you'd killed him."

Tears streamed down her face and he stopped his talking to quickly stoke the fire, pour what water had melted from the plastic jug into the pot and set it on top to boil. When the fire caught, he returned to her side. "You didn't kill Rick. And it took my father's friend to force me to face the real issues. Yes, I was angry at you because you lived and Rick didn't. It tore me apart because, damn it, I was beginning to care for you. But that's not all.''

She swallowed and stared up at him, her misty eyes wide with sympathy.

Outside, the wind died slightly. He took advantage of the relative quiet around them to finish saying what he needed to say. ''Carter forced me to realize that I hadn't dealt with the end of my marriage and especially not with Rick's death. Mostly because I couldn't fight back like I had by being a police officer in the city that killed my father. Like I had when I came here. I bulldozed my way into your life and tried to make you talk. Those were things I *could* do. But with Rick's death, I couldn't correct the mistakes made. When you told me you'd killed Rick, I knew then that I couldn't fight you because I love you.''

His stomach clenched. ''My father's friend said I was too scared to read the autopsy report. He was right. I hadn't looked at it yet.''

She stared at him, panting lightly, and he was at least thankful his miserable explanation was taking her mind off the contractions. He continued, ''The final autopsy report was clear. Rick died from a blood clot, not shock. Not loss of blood. Not sex. Not anything you did. The doctor in Bosnia had done everything he could. You'd done everything right, too. But a small blood clot must have broken loose and traveled to his brain. It can happen, even in nonlife-threatening injuries.'' He cleared his throat to stop his voice from cracking. ''He didn't suffer.''

A small noise escaped from Sylvie's mouth. "I'm sorry."

He couldn't stop himself from talking. "I still blamed you and that got me thinking. That friend of my father's, his partner, didn't kill Dad. A stoned drug pusher did."

She was crying openly now, the tears streaming down her heated cheeks, one slipping around her bottom lip before sliding down her chin.

He held her. "You taught me how to cope, did you know that? You had tried to let go of your regrets. I thought I needed to know how Rick died to find some kind of closure, so you risked whatever peace you'd found so I could have it."

He pressed his hand on her abdomen, feeling it tighten to a hard mass in one undulating, painful wave. "Breathe, Sylvie, like we learned. In, one, two, three…" He counted for her, as she followed his instructions.

Finally she whispered, "I knew I had to tell you the truth. I couldn't stand to see you suffer anymore. You're right. I was a coward and I was scared. But I did everything I could. I'm just hoping that we're not going to lose this baby like we lost Rick. It's too soon."

Tears sprang into his own eyes. "We won't. The doctor will come soon."

The phone burred in the quiet shack. He let go of Sylvie gently to pick it up where he'd dropped it. "Hello?"

"Jon Cahill? This is Captain McInnis. I'm a doctor with the First Lethbridge Regiment. I'm on my way. Can you give me the mother's status?"

Jon blinked at Sylvie. "Um. She's having hard contractions every few minutes. But she's not due until…?"

"December seventeenth," Sylvie finished for him.

"December seventeenth," he told the doctor. "And

her water broke a while ago.'' He caught Sylvie's stricken look. ''When?''

''A couple of hours ago. Maybe more.'' She tightened. ''I want to push!''

''Don't let her push, Jon!'' the doctor ordered him. ''Not yet. Get her pants off. I want you to tell me if you can see the baby.''

See the baby? What? ''Damn it, Doc, can't you just get here?''

''I'll be there, Jon, but listen, I'm still half an hour away, so you're going to have to help. I hear you're a police officer. Haven't you ever helped deliver a baby?''

''No! Do you know how many hospitals there are in Toronto? I've always managed to get the mom to one in time.''

The doctor chuckled. ''Take off her pants and see if you can see the baby's head.''

With Sylvie's help, he managed to pull her pants free. She settled back against the log, her legs splayed open and Jon swallowed hard.

They were going to have to go this alone. And he'd refused to look at all those pictures Lawrence had found of baby's heads and crowning and deliveries.

''Jon?'' The doctor interrupted his growing horror. ''Jon, feel her abdomen. Can you indent the skin above the navel any during a contraction?''

He did as he was asked. ''No.''

''Okay. Look down at the labia, Jon. That's where the baby will come out. Can you see the top of the head?''

He couldn't. That had to be a good sign. ''No.''

''Okay. Do you have latex gloves? Can you wash up?''

He had a first-aid kit in the car. After racing out to retrieve it, he returned. Sylvie was panting hard through another contraction.

"Jon?" The doctor's tinny voice hit him.

He grabbed the phone. "Yeah?"

"Got the gloves on?"

"Yeah."

"Is it warm in there?"

"*I'm* sweating." He'd tried to make a joke, but it didn't work.

"The important thing to remember is to keep the baby warm, should it come before we get there. A coat, shirt, anything, even tin foil if you have it. Keep the baby's head covered, but not its face."

Sylvie groaned. Wiping his face on his shoulder, Jon looked down. There had been a distinctive change down there. Rounded like. With tufts of soft dark hair.

"The head is coming, Doc! Hurry up!"

"Okay. Tell her to pant, not to push through her next contraction. Let's let the head deliver between the contractions. This will help her not to tear. Be prepared to support the head. I want you to push gently on the skin below where the head is coming. Gently but firmly."

Kneeling down, Jon cradled the phone between his cheek and shoulder. With a deep breath, he reached forward. The skin below a bloodied tuft of dark hair felt hot and tight, stretched beyond what was humanly possible.

"I've never delivered a baby before, Doc," he reminded him. "It was always a point of pride to know I was five minutes away from a hospital, anywhere in Toronto."

"Guess what, Dorothy, you aren't in Kansas anymore. Okay, how's the mum?"

He looked up at Sylvie. "Okay?"

"I'm going to push, damn it! Right now!"

The doctor heard her. "Tell her to hold and pant! Tell her to wait until the contraction is done and then she can give it a good push. Tell her, Jon!"

He told her. Her furious panting cut through the still air like a hot knife through butter.

With one hand on her hard abdomen, and the other at the ready, he waited until the contraction passed. "Now," he told her.

"Arrgg!"

A tiny bloodied head slipped through and into his hand. He dropped the phone. "It's here, Doc! The head!"

"Good!" the doctor yelled out. "Pick up the phone, Jon! And hold the baby's head up. Nice and gently."

He did.

"Can you see the cord?"

He searched gingerly. "No."

The baby turned his head, gliding his squat nose along Sylvie's glistening thigh.

"Okay, Jon, listen. The baby will turn its head. I want you to support it. Ask Sylvie to hold her pushing through the next contraction, then push firmly, but not hard. The upper shoulder should come out first."

"It's out."

"Good. Tilt the head up slightly. As soon as the lower shoulder's out, the body will slip out *really* fast. Hold the head with one hand and get ready to hold the rest of the body with the other. Be careful, it's going to be slippery. Get close and use your lap."

His nephew slipped out just as the doctor had said. An incredibly small, red and very angry little baby boy.

"He's out! Sylvie, it's a boy!"

"Jon, put him on his back and cover him with the cleanest thing you have."

Jon wrapped him in Sylvie's jacket. "Doc, what do I do now?"

"With a clean cloth, wipe his nose and mouth. Gently.

Lift up his bum slightly to help drain his nose and mouth. Is he breathing?''

"I don't know." Jon's heart lodged in his throat. *Come on, little Rickie, breathe. Breathe!*

"Rub his back, Jon, and keep his head lowered and slightly downward. He may not start to breathe on his own."

Jon rubbed his back. "Come on, breathe for Uncle Jon."

The baby let out a tiny little gasp and squawk. Relief washed through Jon, and he looked up at Sylvie. The phone slipped down his arm to hit the floor again. Sylvie laughed.

The baby let out another squawk, followed by a louder, stronger and angrier cry.

"Jon! Jon!"

He retrieved the phone. "He's angry, but he's crying, Doc!"

And so am I, he thought. Through his own tears, he looked up at Sylvie. She sank back, tired and sweating and glowing, with her own streams of tears glittering in the firelight. God, she looked great.

"Good," the doctor said. "Excellent. Wrap him up so only his face is exposed. Put him on Sylvie's abdomen."

He did as the doctor ordered. "He's perfect, Sylvie. Like his mother." Jon leaned forward and kissed her firmly on the lips. "I love you. I want to be your husband and I want to be a father to this baby."

Sylvie wrapped one arm around the baby. She looked up at him. "You're already his father, Jon."

The doctor yelled out, "There's going to be another hard contraction and having the baby on her abdomen will help. How's the cord, Jon?"

He scooped up his phone, finding it hard to hold while

his hands were so wet and bloodied. "White and just lying there. It's long."

"It should be."

"Do I have to cut it?"

"No. Don't cut it. I'll be there soon. It's messy, but it's perfectly safe to keep the cord and placenta with the baby for several hours. Now find another cloth and get ready to guide the placenta out as it delivers. Don't pull it! I want you to wrap it up in the cloth and lay it on top of the baby's stomach. Get Sylvie to push through the next contraction."

Jon blinked and waited. And sweated. Above him, the baby cried and above the baby, Sylvie leaned forward. Her arms protecting the baby, she pushed hard.

The doctor yelled out, "We're here, Jon! I see the shack."

By the time Jon turned his head, the doctor was barreling in the door.

Chapter 20

"The clinic said you could have had the ceremony right there in the maternity ward, you know." Lawrence grimaced as he loosened his buttoned-up collar. "It would have been good to have Rick, Jr., at your wedding."

Jon loosened his own tie. "Then you wouldn't get to wear your good suit."

"Why do you think I suggested it?"

Overhearing them, Sylvie walked up and looped her arm with Jon's. "Rickie's kind of busy right now, getting strong enough to leave that incubator." She smiled up at Jon. "I promised the nurse I'd come straight back after the wedding. She wants me to try breast-feeding him again."

"Breast is best," Lawrence quoted. "But for me, punch is best." He peered into his empty glass.

Sylvie watched Lawrence head toward the punch bowl,

where her father and Andrea were chatting with Major Tirouski.

She'd been a bit wary when she'd seen him standing at the back of the church, in his dress greens, closest to the aisle and the exit. But he nodded briefly, almost in approval.

The major had taken them aside that morning and, to Sylvie's surprise, apologized for everything that had gone wrong. The investigation had revealed that a young German liaison officer, sympathetic to one rogue band of guerrillas, had arranged for the incorrect grid references and subsequent ambush. He was immediately repatriated to Germany for a court martial.

Setting that aside, Sylvie glanced around until she spotted her childhood friends there, too. Soft-hearted Denise stood tall and beautiful, crying, while the shorter, wiry Lucy thrust tissue after tissue into her hands. Someday, the trio would go back up to the lookout. Someday when they'd all found happiness, like Sylvie had.

Her wedding had been hastily planned, by Andrea of course, but it had been a smashing success. Sylvie had only just been released from the clinic herself, yesterday, and she'd left Andrea to handle all the details, even pick out her wedding gown. She smoothed down the pale-pink silk dress. She'd never have considered such a feminine style, but the dress was…well, pretty.

Jon had insisted on marrying her now, before he had to return to Toronto where he'd fill in his request for a transfer to the Royal Canadian Mounted Police, out here in Trail. He already had the chief of police's approval.

She felt Jon's arm slip free of hers and loop around her waist. He leaned forward to bury his nose in her short hair, styled today by Andrea. "Thank you," he whispered.

Pulling away slightly, she smiled. "For what?"

He looked into the distance. "Where do you want me to begin? For fighting back for me? I've dealt with people who've been desperate, too, and they've given up. You didn't."

"Out in the line shack? I didn't want you to lose little Rickie, not after all you'd gone through." She sighed. "Before that, I wondered if I was going to die along with him."

He gripped her, and she knew he didn't want to think about that. "When I got home, I had to face all those boxes. All of Rick's life rolled into a few barrack boxes and cartons and a duffel bag."

She rubbed his arm. "I wish I'd been there to help you."

"It was something I had to do myself." He glanced around before pulling her into the closest corner. "As it was it took me months to get to it. It wasn't until I opened the first box, did I understand your courage. You say you were a coward that night in Bosnia. And we both thought what you did was a mistake. Maybe some people would agree, but I don't anymore. You were scared and desperate, but I wouldn't call anything a mistake that brought me to you."

He glanced down at her hands, to the ring he'd put on her finger less than an hour ago. His voice dropped, and he had to grip her fingers to stop his own hand from shaking. "Not even Rick's death. I miss him like crazy. I wish he hadn't died. But he was an adult, and he knew the risks. And you tried to cope with a situation that no one is ever fully prepared for. I know. I train constantly for just such situations. A person can train and act automatically, but you're never really prepared to face death. You just cope the best way you can. I can't blame you for wanting to find something good in all that bad. It's natural.''

He dropped a kiss on her furrowing brow. "He died in the line of duty. I remember when he called to say he was slated for Bosnia. He said someone had to go there and keep the peace. He said there were too many innocent children over there who needed that peace.''

Her heart swelled. Jon was thinking of Rickie, too. One more innocent child who needed peace and love.

"Are you ready to be Rickie's father?''

He smiled and the pensive moment passed. "As ready as I am to be your husband.'' He eyed her speculatively, one dark eyebrow lifted. "Are you ready to be my wife, Mrs. Sylvie Cahill?''

There was that silky tone again. He just said her name exactly the way he'd said it that early-June day, right there in Trail. And it still conjured up visions of hot moonless nights and smooth, knowing caresses.

"Umm. You've never spent a winter in Alberta, have you? This isn't *balmy* Toronto. We'll see how ready you are for the cold.'' She pulled him close, pressing herself against him with suggestive intimacy as she wiggled her eyebrows. "And those long winter nights.''

He crushed her to him, and she could feel how ready he was. The sounds of the church hall faded away as she savored his unspoken intention.

Sadness had brought them together, and they'd searched for some kind of closure. Who would have guessed that their closure had been found in their mutual love?

She pulled Jon down for a hot, smiling kiss. Maybe Rick or little Rickie. Maybe.

* * * * *

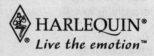

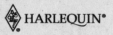

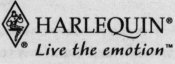

If you enjoyed what you just read,
then we've got an offer you can't resist!

Take 2 bestselling
love stories FREE!

Plus get a FREE surprise gift!

Clip this page and mail it to Silhouette Reader Service™

IN U.S.A.
3010 Walden Ave.
P.O. Box 1867
Buffalo, N.Y. 14240-1867

IN CANADA
P.O. Box 609
Fort Erie, Ontario
L2A 5X3

YES! Please send me 2 free Silhouette Intimate Moments® novels and my free
surprise gift. After receiving them, if I don't wish to receive anymore, I can return
the shipping statement marked cancel. If I don't cancel, I will receive 6 brand-new
novels every month, before they're available in stores! In the U.S.A., bill me at the
bargain price of $4.24 plus 25¢ shipping and handling per book and applicable
sales tax, if any*. In Canada, bill me at the bargain price of $4.99 plus 25¢ shipping
and handling per book and applicable taxes**. That's the complete price and a
savings of at least 10% off the cover prices—what a great deal! I understand that
accepting the 2 free books and gift places me under no obligation ever to buy any
books. I can always return a shipment and cancel at any time. Even if I never buy
another book from Silhouette, the 2 free books and gift are mine to keep forever.

245 SDN DZ9A
345 SDN DZ9C

Name	(PLEASE PRINT)	
Address	Apt.#	
City	State/Prov.	Zip/Postal Code

Not valid to current Silhouette Intimate Moments® subscribers.

Want to try two free books from another series?
Call 1-800-873-8635 or visit www.morefreebooks.com.

* Terms and prices subject to change without notice. Sales tax applicable in N.Y.
** Canadian residents will be charged applicable provincial taxes and GST.
  All orders subject to approval. Offer limited to one per household].
  ® are registered trademarks owned and used by the trademark owner and its licensee.

INMOM04R   ©2004 Harlequin Enterprises Limited

SPOTLIGHT

"Debra Webb's fast-paced thriller will make you shiver in passion and fear...."—*Romantic Times*

Dying To Play

Debra Webb

When FBI agent Trace Callahan arrives in Atlanta to investigate a baffling series of multiple homicides, deputy chief of detectives Elaine Jentzen isn't prepared for the immediate attraction between them. And as they hunt to find the killer known as the Gamekeeper, it seems that Trace is singled out as his next victim...unless Elaine can stop the Gamekeeper before it's too late.

Available January 2005.

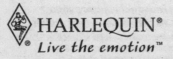

Live the emotion™

Exclusive Bonus Features:
Author Interview
Sneak Preview...
and more!

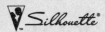

COMING NEXT MONTH

SIMCNM0105

INTIMATE MOMENTS